T0116829

The Absence of Purity

T. O. Stallings

AuthorHouse™
1663 Liberty Drive
Bloomington, IN 47403
www.authorhouse.com
Phone: 1-800-839-8640

First published by AuthorHouse   5/11/2011

ISBN: 978-1-4567-6420-3 (e)
ISBN: 978-1-4567-6421-0 (hc)
ISBN: 978-1-4567-6422-7 (sc)

Library of Congress Control Number: 2011906132

Printed in the United States of America

CHAPTER ONE

Silhouetted by the rays of a dying moon the house stood cold, silent, and uninviting. Standing in the thin layer of snow which blanketed the ground, his rigid posture mimicked the coldness of the structure. As time slipped past, his lack of motion sent the beginnings of numbness into the bottom of his feet. Still he remained immobile. His mind played out different scenarios, all of which he finally concluded, would leave signs of his presence. After all the planning, the hours of waiting, and the mental exhaustion, tell-tale signs were not acceptable.

Someone on the second floor flicked a light switch. Through the blindless window he saw the movement and it mesmerized him. Tall and graceful, like a ballerina the naked figure made its way across the room, through the door and, turning on the necessary switches to light the way, into the hall. He knew the route. He had walked it hundreds of times in his mind. He knew the location of every switch, every discarded piece of clothing that would be navigated around, and every squeak of the flooring. Soon downstairs lights would be illuminating the interior, the power of their brightness casting shadows on the immediate outside vicinity.

A less organized individual would have retreated in fear of

detection. His courage was in the knowledge that from his vantage point he was invisible. Daylight was more than two hours away and his confidence kept him glued to his position. Two hours could be a lifetime. Two hours could be the beginning of something truly wonderful. It could also be an end.

Watching the activity inside the house birthed images in his brain and the familiarity of past actions shrouded him in an unrepentant arousal. All the memories of the past were unleashed and for a moment he shuddered with his thoughts. Another time, he told himself. Another night when circumstances were perfect, he would return and then the pictures he envisioned could, and would become reality.

Slowly, forcing his stiff limbs to move, he stepped backwards, not wanting to lose sight of the house. Finally he turned. Breathing heavily he walked with his head down, his eyes focused on the ground. He had parked two miles from his hiding point and when he arrived he started the engine and turned the heat to full. Lighting a cigarette he noticed his hands shaking. After the times before they had shaken violently and he took it as a positive omen.

Finished with the cigarette he held it between his thumb and forefinger out the window, rolling it back and forth knocking the ash to the ground. What was left of the butt he placed in his jacket pocket. Placing the car in drive he eased his way onto the road, slowly increasing his speed. Ten minutes later he turned on the headlights and maneuvered the vehicle onto the highway. At that time of the morning traffic was sparse and it afforded him time to replay the past hours in his mind.

Parking in his driveway while the sky was still awakening to a new dawn he exited the vehicle and moved quietly up the steps of the porch and into the foyer. The house was silent. Stripping off his footwear and jacket, he walked in stocking feet to the mudroom where he stripped his clothing and tossed them into the washing machine. From the mud room he made his way through the house, up the stairs and into the bedroom. In the dimness of the predawn light he could make out the form sleeping under the blankets .Gently he pulled back the bed linens and stretched out beside her. Within minutes he was asleep.

Within the house the day's activities were limited. A product of habit, the early wake up in the darkness meant nothing more sinister than having extra time to prepare the standard weekend fare of pancakes and waffles for breakfast. Showers came afterwards as did the accomplishment of tasks delegated for weekends. As was their sacrament, weekend afternoons were reserved for bedroom intimacy. Before five they again dressed. Venturing out doors they drove to a nearby store, made a few select purchases, and then returned to the house. To those they encountered during their trip they greeted with smiles and cordial civility. Not habitually inclined towards idle chatter and adhering to their self-imposed cloistered lifestyle, the few words they spoke were gracious and friendly. Favoring the accomplishment of their tasks as swiftly as possible they did not linger.

Stopping at the end of their driveway they retrieved the mail from the metal box prior to continuing to the house. Noting they had received a movie and letter from Germany they continued to the house. Finding homes for their newest acquisitions they moved about the house without distractions. Saturday evening dinner was a simple casual affair. A cold meal served with copious quantities of wine. The trio conversed with the ease of humor and familiarity of intimacy.

The male was of average height with brownish hair and a lean but physical frame. The woman was taller than the male. She too was of average height. Neither thin nor fat her body showed the toning of the regiment of exercise in which they all participated. Despite her obvious good looks she was often teased, in good nature, by the other two for her smaller than average breasts and her slightly enlarged buttocks. The girl was always referred to as beautiful. Blemish free skin enhanced a sumptuous figure which was further embellished with the tightness of her clothing. Collectively they enjoyed her ability to catch the attention of all who met her.

The note which accompanied the movie was brief, stating only wishes for their enjoyment. Seated together on the large sofa they watched the home made video without comment. Filmed in black and white the movie lasted a few minutes short of two hours. As it rewound the suggestion was made to again view the film the following afternoon. Nodding heads agreed. Making the nightly rounds of securing doors and turning off lights the trio made their way up the stairs into the bedroom. Not bothering with the lights they assisted each other with undressing. Soon they were sprawled across the bed indulging in the passions the movie inflamed. When all three were gratified they extinguished the light and drifted into the sleep of contentment

The day dragged by. He busied himself with mundane chores in the barn and the yard. The day's sun melted the remains of the snow but its temporary warmth was replaced by a cold wind. The forecast for the night called for a freeze. In the afternoon he checked his backpack. Satisfied it contained everything he would need he spent the rest of the day pretending to read and watch the news.

"I have to go to Asheville tonight," he announced at the dinner table.

"What time?" His wife looked up from her plate.

"About ten or so," he responded.

"It's going to be cold. You'd better wear your heavy parka."

"I'll be okay," he said, a slight sneer touching his lips.

"When will you be back?" Her eyes rested on his face.

"In the morning if everything goes alright." He pushed his plate away from him. "If you could make me a thermos of coffee." He said it more as a command than a request. Standing up he left her sitting at the table. Alone, she finished her meal then cleaned the kitchen. After preparing the thermos she turned off all the lights and went to the bedroom.

He was there laying on the bed, half dressed, eyes closed with his forearm over his face. "You asleep?' she asked.

"No."

"Coffee is on the table in the kitchen."

He moved his arm so he could see her as she undressed. The process captured his attention and he counted the strokes as she brushed her shoulder length hair. Without bringing attention to himself he exhaled slowly. The site of her nakedness still excited him and for a moment he considered satisfying the excitement. No, he reasoned. He needed his energy for what was to come this evening. The morning would be more suitable. As she climbed under the blankets he turned and kissed her. "Time to go," he whispered, and swung his feet off the bed onto the floor.

He dressed silently in the dark. Retrieving the thermos from the kitchen and the backpack from the barn he tossed them in the front seat. Taking a deep breath he started the car and drove into the night. The dashboard clock glowed 10:05. The radio, turned down to a barely audible level, accompanied him during the drive.

He parked in the same place as the night before. Out of the vehicle he locked it and took several minutes to scan the area. Satisfied he was alone he shuffled off to his hiding place. Once there he stood quietly watching the house. One light was visible on the second floor. He waited. Within minutes the light went out. He continued to wait.

After an hour he stepped from the trees which shielded him. Stealthily he walked across the field and the yard. The temperature had dipped into the low twenties yet he detected a bead of perspiration across his brow which the slight breeze did not evaporate. At the door he waited again, ears straining to hear any noise or movement. There was none. From his backpack he retrieved his tools and within seconds he was standing inside the house.

CHAPTER TWO

Founded in 1852, and named after the former president Andrew, Jackson County, North Carolina is situated in the northeast corner of the state. With an ancestry of almost an equal mixture of English, Irish, German, and Scot-Irish, with local Native American descendants from the Cherokee nation thrown in, its land area totals nearly 500 square miles. The terrain is heavily wooded and mountainous. The county's fifteen townships boast names like Balsam, Cullowhee, Dillsboro, Webster, and Sylva. A poor county, the average income remains below the national level. Although there are three major roadways in the county, the Smokey Mountain Expressway in the north which runs east to west, state road 107 which runs north to south, and US 64 in the southern part of the county which also runs east to west, there is also a plethora of back roads which zigzag across the landscape. To travelers unfamiliar with the secondary roads and dead end trails, the potential to become disoriented or lost is quiet real.

Sunday mornings in Jackson County are historically a quiet time. For the vast majority of the population it is a time for family breakfast, for preparing for morning worship services at one of the many churches, or for lounging about reading the paper. Local retailers do not open until churches are closed. A Sunday morning in a winter January is expected to be quiet and Aaron Tidwell was one of those who partook of the opportunity of spending extra time in bed. The phone disturbed his tranquility. "Yes," he said trying to stifle a yawn.

The words, more than the voice, jolted him awake. Listening intently he nodded saying, "Okay" and replaced the receiver. Jumping from bed he dressed hurriedly in the first clothes he could put his hands on. Stopping at his dresser he opened the top drawer. Staring back at him from their resting place were his badge and his nine millimeter automatic. The badge went into his shirt pocket and the weapon into its holster. Carrying the cup of coffee his wife made for him he kissed her good-bye and went out into the coldness of the morning. Instinctively he knew it would be a very long day.

Pulling onto the Great Smokey Mountains Expressway and turning west, he flipped on the cruisers blue lights but left the siren off. Easily passing the limited number of other vehicles he navigated his way to Thomas Valley Ranch Road, headed north and, slowing so he wouldn't miss the turn he drove onto an unnamed dirt lane. A marked patrol car was parked at the side. Waving to the officer he continued up the lane, through the jungle of pines, and emerged into an acre clearing. Parking so he would not block access to the lane he shut down the lights and exited the car.

The front lawn was littered with vehicles. He counted three fire trucks, two ambulances, and another four patrol cars. From what he could see the wood deck on the front of the house was nearly destroyed by the fire, its carcass still shedding whiffs of smoke. To the left of the deck and up the exterior of the two story home to the roof line he could see where the fire charred the logs but not destroyed them. Where windows once protected the interior from the elements there were gaping holes. If knocked out by the firemen or having exploded due to the fire he couldn't tell. On the right side of the deck the flames had licked their way upward but not reached the second story.

"Glad to see you Aaron." The greeting came from James Woody.

"Jim," Aaron responded to the fire marshal. "Looks like you had a hell of a fire."

"Fires out now. We're just here to make sure there is no flashback." He removed his headgear and ran his hand through his thinning gray hair. "It was definitely arson and I've already called the boys at state to send an investigator. But that's not why you're here. We found three bodies on the second floor."

Tidwell looked at the fireman. "Forensics been called?" Jim nodded yes. "Fire kill them?" A shaking head said no. "Okay then, let's have a look."

"You can't go up the front, it's not safe. Go around to the back. Those steps didn't get the full blast from the fire. They're safe enough to use."

Deputy Roger Sherman was standing at the bottom of the back porch steps and four other deputies stood a few feet away engaged in quiet conversation. Tidwell nodded to Sherman as he made his way up and in. The back door led into the kitchen area. Standing amidst the charred smoky interior he knew immediately the crime scene, or what little remained of it, was unavoidably compromised by the necessary actions of the firefighters. The stench of smoke attacked his nostrils causing him to sneeze. Pulling a handkerchief from his pocket he covered his nose.

Between the fire, the smoke, and the high pressure water used to extinguish the blaze, the downstairs resembled the aftermath of a tornado strike. Groaning, he picked his path through the rubble.

When new the house was like hundreds of others he had seen during the course of his career. Downstairs was split between a living room, a dining room, kitchen, and laundry room. Upstairs contained the three bedrooms and two baths. A deck was attached to both the front and the back.

Now, standing in the front room which he guessed used to be the living room because of the remains of a television, he was convinced the house was a complete loss. On the opposite side was another room in the same condition. Between the two rooms was the stairs to the second floor. Another uniformed deputy stood at the bottom. Aaron nodded to him and made his way upward.

At the top of the stairs the smell of smoke was not as intense and he stuffed his handkerchief back into his jacket pocket. Pulling on latex gloves he stood motionless taking in the layout of the second floor. The hall formed a tee at the stairway landing. To the left he could see three closed doors. At first glance they appeared to have been spared the heat of the flames. To the right the single door was open. He moved toward it unsure of what to expect.

The room had filled with smoke and to reduce the smoke someone opened the windows. The cold breeze of the morning air exploited the openings, filtering itself inward, cooling the room. Against the back wall stood the king size bed, to the right a door leading to a bath. The left wall supported a long dresser and opposite it on the right, a tall bureau. The wood floor was partially covered with a rug of some kind of animal skin and discarded clothing. The night stands on either side of the bed were cluttered with glasses, paper back books and magazines. The beds linens had been removed and discarded in a heap by the right side. Any pillows that might have lived on the bed were missing. The bodies were on the bed.

The male's hands were tied to the headboard, his feet to the footboard. He had been shot in the forehead by a small caliber pistol at close range. The skin was burned by the residue and blast of the shot. Blood, mixed with bone fragments and brain matter lay spattered across the head board and the wall. Like the two females he was naked. The older of the two females was laying on her right side, her head down by the male victim's feet. There was a minuscule bruise on the side of her face. Her lips were covered in bright red lipstick. Her eye lids were closed. He could see no stab marks or gun shot wounds. The youngest female was laying face up. She too was positioned with her head next to the male's feet. Her open eyes stared blankly at Tidwell as he peered over her body. Red lipstick covered her lips as well. Her legs were spread apart, and an artificial rose lay between them. "What in the name of God happened here?" he said under his breath.

Forensics arrived as he was finishing his inspection of the other rooms. "I want pictures from every angle and of everything, before the bodies are moved," he instructed. This, he acknowledged to himself, could be a career breaker. "Tell the coroner we need a rape kit on the two females and toxicology on all three. Dust everything on the second floor even though I don't think you'll find any prints." Turning towards the hall he left them to their task.

Back outside he found the fire marshal talking on his radio. Waiting until he had completed his transmissions he produced a cigar from his jacket and biting off the end and spitting it out he jabbed the cigar into his mouth. "You need a light?" Jim asked.

"No, I just chew on them. Trying to quit you know, but chewing on them helps me think. You have a point of origin for the fire yet?"

"Not really. If I had to guess I'd say there were two; one in the front by the deck and one in the back by the kitchen."

"You have an accelerant?"

"Hell, Aaron! The varnished beams of the ceiling are natural accelerant. But my guess, and my noses guess would be sterno."

"Who reported the fire?" Tidwell rolled the cigar between the tips of his fingers.

"Driver, passing by, saw the smoke, called it in."

"House kind of sits back from view. Not so easy to see anything up here." Tidwell put the cigar in his mouth. Slowly he looked down the lane then back at the house. "You got the name of the good citizen?" he asked. "They must have x-ray vision to have seen this fire."

Jim shook his head. "Dispatch should. I'll get it for you."

Thanking him Tidwell retreated to his car. Aaron Tidwell was no stranger to violence. He arrived in Jackson County by way of walking a beat in New Orleans where he worked his way from uniform patrol to a place in the detectives. It wasn't an easy journey. He had been shot at, stabbed, punched, and during one particularly unpleasant domestic dispute, battered with a rolling pin. Add the bumps and bruises to the rampant corruption on the force, and after ten years, he had had enough. Yet the countless murders he'd seen and the nightly depraved sickness he'd witnessed in a city with limited morals, he confessed to himself, had not prepared him for today. The scene had not made him physically ill but saddened his heart. What transpired within the confines of that room was something he wasn't sure he wanted to know in detail, but understood, in the end, he would be forced to know every repulsive second.

Picking up the mike of the radio he called dispatch. "Better call the Sheriff," he said after they responded. "I'll wait for him here. And after that you should call Joe Sawyer at SBI. His number is in my office. We're going to need his help on this one."

With the cigar firmly clamped between his teeth he frowned

staring down at the ground. Lost in thought he didn't realize the sun broke through the clouds and the air was warming.

The sky was darkening before the bodies, zipped inside the black coroner's bags were removed from the scene. The Sheriff, a small man with thinning hair and spectacles arrived within an hour after his presence was requested. Dressed for morning church services he looked out of place among the tired and soot covered firemen who still roamed the grounds. Next to the tall and muscular Tidwell, the Sheriff, standing quietly with his hands clasped behind his back listening to the preliminary report, looked more like a wayward trespasser being scolded than a superior questioning a subordinate.

Between the two of them they outlined the immediate steps to be taken in the investigation and determined which facts would be kept from the media. Supplied with the name of the person who reported the fire the Sheriff used Tidwell's radio to dispatch a patrol car to pick up the Good Samaritan for questioning. Other deputies were set to work finding the locations of registered sex offenders. They would all be required to come in for interviewing. After satisfying himself he was acquainted with what facts they knew to that point the Sheriff departed leaving Tidwell in charge of the scene.

The arson investigator arrived by noon and automatically took command. The transfer of jurisdiction went into effect quietly, as soon as he drove onto the property. In North Carolina the State Bureau of Investigation, an arm of the Attorney General's office, is responsible for all suspected arsons. A half hour later Joe Sawyer from the criminal branch of SBI arrived.

Five years older than Tidwell, they had been in law enforcement the same amount of time. Before Aaron was walking a beat Sawyer was attending the University of North Carolina, majoring in criminology with a minor in psychology. He had gone straight into the bureau after graduating. His success was slow but steady and his college minor enabled him to become a trusted profiler for the state. They first met at an Asheville seminar and Sawyer instantly liked the dark hair New Orleans transplant with his brooding eyes and his soft calming voice that hinted of a southern drawl. Never having actually worked any cases together the two remained in contact through correspondence and the exchange of Christmas cards.

Accompanying Tidwell, Sawyer entered the house and what was now called the crime room. The bodies had slipped from limberness into the rigor of death. Bending over to place his face close to each body he said, "This is not the first time he's done this."

"Are you sure?" asked Tidwell.

"He's no rookie," was the reply. "A small room with a lot of individuals in the middle of the night, probably with limited lighting, and no forensic evidence, I'm guessing now, would leave me to believe this is the work of someone very methodical and meticulous."

Tidwell sighed. "Have you seen any thing like this before?"

"Not in the Carolina's," Sawyer answered.

"I guess it's not possible it was a random act," Tidwell said hopefully.

"Doubt it." Sawyer stood up. "Have you identified them yet?"

"The Cromwell family; moved here about six months ago. The man is Adam - husband of Joyce, the older of the two females, and father of Amanda. She was fourteen."

"What's that smell?" Sawyer once again leaned over the bodies of the females, his nose within inches of their skin. He inhaled deeply several times. "Bleach? It smells like bleach."

"That about kills any chance of DNA." Tidwell sighed.

"Have the bodies taken to Asheville," said Sawyer. "We'll do all the lab work."

Sawyer's eyes lingered over the bodies. "There are several contradictions here," he said. "Violence ended the man's life. Gunshot wound to the head. The older female, more than likely posed after death, but no sign of violence. Hell, her eyes are even closed. That's an act of humanity. The girl was posed as well, I'm sure, but her eyes were left open and a rose was placed between her legs. A rose is often confused with a symbol of love between two people. Some people see it as a symbol of purity. Fragile and delicate as young girls are supposed to be."

"You think he was trying to save her from some imaginary harm?" Tidwell asked. Sawyer shrugged as they left the room.

The pair walked back out to Tidwell's car. "We can't tell if there was forced entry because of the fire," said Tidwell. "Whoever did this was trying to cover their tracks."

"I don't think so," Sawyer injected. "The fire was his way of making sure the bodies were found today. Ironic, isn't it, that the crime room was the least damaged room. He's not trying to hide anything."

"What do you mean?" Tidwell asked.

"Understand this Aaron. Whoever did this - as sick and twisted as we may think their mind is," he paused to take a cigarette from his pocket and light it. After inhaling deeply he continued, the smoke escaping his mouth as he spoke. "That person is just as smart as me and you or anyone else. Hell, maybe smarter. I'm just thinking out loud right now, okay. This wasn't random. This wasn't the first time. On the surface there appears to be no forensic evidence. And if I am sure this wasn't his first time; I have to be equally positive it won't be his last."

"Why do you say that?" Worry swept Tidwell's face.

"Rookie killers always make mistakes. We may not always pick up on their screw ups right away, but it's always there. Only experienced killers, through trial and error, have perfected an absence of clues. The only way to achieve experience is to kill again. The only way to stay skilled is to continue to kill." He lit another cigarette and let the smoke escape through his nose. "But I'll tell you this right now," he said slowly, his voice lower. "If we don't solve this thing, our careers will be just as dead as the victims in that bedroom.

CHAPTER THREE

He awoke ravenous. His wife prepared a large breakfast of eggs, sausage, and pancakes. They showered together, their naked closeness ending in a frantic chaotic form of love making. Afterwards they dressed and prepared for church. He promised her right after they met he would accompany her on Sundays. He always lived up to the promise. As he started the car the sun struggled to achieve its full brilliance. They drove the ten miles in silence.

Listening to the sermon he willed his mind to block out the events of the previous night. The effort was painful. The fantasy world in his mind that he often visited was a better, happier existence than reality. He found that world while still a teenager and he spent as much time in it as possible. At the completion of the services he escorted his wife out, shaking the ministers hand while telling him how much they enjoyed his words..

Parking the car in the driveway he turned and asked, "Have you thought about us moving?"

"Oh, honey," she responded. "We've only been here less than two years. You've got a good job and we're happy. Besides, where would we go?"

"Maybe somewhere that's always warm. Sometimes I get tired of the cold." He leaned across the seat and kissed her on the check. "It was just a thought."

Inside he changed his clothes, opting for the casual sweat pants and shirt. Flipping on the television in the living room he found a football game and settled his body on the sofa. At some point she joined him, snuggling next to him. Automatically he placed his arm around her and stroked her hair, his mind neither on her or the game. His mind had retreated to his safe place.

He was lost in the memories of the past, his childhood, his first time, that first rush of joy he experienced. Then there was the power. Perhaps that was the real satisfaction. The powers of control while all others actions were unquestioned and resulted in immediate obedience. Every hint of a suggestion was carried out, in order to gain his approval. It flushed his skin with goose bumps of delight. He freed them from their false modesty, their society imposed inhibitions which limited their naturalness, and in doing so he allowed them a glimpse, if only briefly, of what true freedom could be. Their arrival in paradise was breathtaking. Spiritual in its righteousness. Even in the restricted light of a bedroom illuminated by candles, the utopia etched on their faces could only be witnessed. Words, however eloquent, were inadequate to capture the essence of their ecstasy.

But in the end his genius saw through their lies. They were consumed with evil and instead of accepting and being grateful for their liberation they were mocking him. Evil must be destroyed or it would grow. Like a corrupting cancer they needed to be cleansed to be made whole. Knowing he would have to punish them he wept. They misunderstood his tears. He scolded them, revealing he knew their attempt to deceive him. Exposed, they retreated into their insecurities, pleading for mercy. Despite their attempts he knew he needed to remain strong. It was mandated they be freed from their evil so they could be saved. Understanding they were to be punished brought on the hysteria. Their punishment brought silence.

"Did you hear that?" his wife asked. He snapped back to the present.

"Hear what?" Her question forced him to focus on her.

"That news flash - three people were found dead in their Jackson County home."

He squinted at the television. "Wonder what happened?"

"That's so sad." She leaned her head on his shoulder. He pulled her closer, drinking in the smell of her hair. She was so different than him. Shoulder length red hair, angular, freckled face, quick to smile displaying almost perfect teeth, and a vibrant, naïve trust of others. He kissed the top of her head and let his hands roam down her side until they rested on her thin leg.

She was raised in the mountains of Colorado by poor uneducated parents and it had been a struggle for them to get her a basic education. She dropped out of school at the age of twelve to help around the house. Being a child of limited experience, when they met she thought him worldly, the smartest man she had ever knew, and his modest income a guarantee of financial security. He was convinced she was an angel sent to aid him in his mission. It hadn't taken much to woo her or, after a reasonable period of courtship and a few promises, to talk her parents into allowing her to move in with him. She was three months shy of her sixteenth birthday. He was thirty-one. Under his tutelage she had grown into the perfect wife; or, he reasoned, the closest thing to it.

CHAPTER FOUR

Mother Nature turned a cold shoulder to the area and allowed a biting wind to whip through the valleys. The worsening weather did little to alleviate Aaron Tidwell's mood. Not having much sleep the night before he settled for coffee to go and left home early, arriving at his office before six. Preliminary reports were on his desk and he started the task of reading and digesting them, temporarily ignoring the Sylva newspaper which dedicated five pages to the story, its headlines blaring "**MURDER IN THE MOUNTAINS.**" There was a picture of the half burned house surrounded by official vehicles and a picture of Tidwell talking with the Sheriff. Funny, he thought, he didn't remember the picture being taken.

The man who reported the fire had been questioned at length by deputies. His movements checked and verified, he was thanked then sent on his way. His name was scratched from the possible suspect pool. Registered sex offenders were being interviewed relatively quickly. Sylva alone had ten within a five mile radius. Six had already been eliminated as possible participants. The seventh, Charlie Reese, was brought in as Tidwell was finishing with the reports. After pouring himself a cup of coffee he entered the interrogation room.

"I'm Detective Tidwell of the Jackson County Sheriff's office," he said taking a seat on the opposite side of the table which separated him from the small skinny man who stared at him. "We need to ask you a few questions, if that's okay." The man nodded. "Do you want a lawyer present?" The man shook his head no. "You understand you are entitled to one? "The man nodded again. "What have you been doing this weekend?"

"Just the normal stuff," he replied, his voice was heavy with the remnants of drinking. "I didn't do nothing really."

"Normal stuff and didn't do nothing. First words out of your mouth are not making me feel warm and fuzzy," Tidwell retorted. "What about Saturday night? What normal stuff were you doing then?"

"Watching the TV." Reese looked down at the table. "That ain't against the law is it?"

"Oh, really. .What did you watch?" Tidwell asked.

"I don't remember." Reese twisted in his chair, obviously uncomfortable. He was awakened from sleep by the deputies who brought him in. Not given much time to dress he was outfitted in a plaid jacket, dirty sweatshirt and blue jeans. His hands were stained with nicotine and his breath had the stench of day old alcohol.

"Don't remember huh?" Tidwell sipped his coffee. "Charlie that could be a problem. You know that don't you? You know what happened don't you?" Tidwell allowed minutes of silence while he continued to sip from his cup. "Okay Charlie, here's the deal. You answer my questions and you go home. You don't answer my questions and we'll hold you for failure to cooperate with the authorities. That is part of your parole conditions isn't it?" Charlie nodded. "What was that? I didn't hear you."

"Yes," Reese said louder.

"Okay, let's start again. Where were you Saturday night?"

"Home, watching TV and," he looked down at the table. "having a few drinks."

"A few drinks huh? You smell like you had more than a few. That's in violation of your parole isn't it? We can send you back for that. Is that what you want, to go back inside?"

Charlie shook his head no. "I didn't do anything. Just a few drinks that's all. I didn't hurt anybody."

The questioning took an hour and a half. Slowly, meticulously, and methodical, Tidwell covered from Saturday morning until the deputies escorted him to the office. In the end Aaron knew the man did not commit the murders. In the end he held Charlie for parole violation, turning him over to the booking officer.

Other interrogations were transpiring while he was interviewing Charlie. By noon all known and registered sex offenders were questioned. As systematically as they had been questioned they were ruled out. The outcome came as no surprise to Tidwell. It would have been too easy. In the back of his mind a premonition of gloom began to ferment.

When the Sheriff entered his office Tidwell was reviewing what they knew about the victims. "Nice picture, Tidwell," the Sheriff said sarcastically. "County's hell bent to get this thing over. Phones have been ringing off the hook. A million questions which I don't have answers for," the Sheriff blurted out.

"It's going to get worse before it gets better," Tidwell said. "Usual suspects have been cleared."

"The County fathers want a hotline set up for tips. What's your thought?"

"Not my call." Tidwell said shrugging his shoulders. Tip hot lines, he knew, were a double edged sword. Historically they were inundated with thousands of useless calls requiring massive resources to investigate. But the right anonymous call would crack the case wide open.

"SBI got anything yet?" the Sheriff asked.

"Preliminary. Autopsies won't be complete for some days yet and drug tests will take a few days too. Arson boys, although they think they know, they have nothing conclusive yet. It all takes time." The phone rang. Joe Sawyer was on the other end. Tidwell listened without speaking then hung the receiver in the cradle. "That's what I was afraid of."

"What are you afraid of Tidwell?" asked the Sheriff.

"That was Sawyer from SBI. He ran a national check for unsolved similar crimes. There are two; one in Colorado and one in Arkansas. Same MO. He's put in a request for copies of their files. We should have them in a couple of days."

"Serial killer? In Jackson County?" The Sheriff sounded dumbfounded as he watched Tidwell nod. "Damn it, that's not possible!" He wiped his hand across his face. "This is a sleepy village with good honest working people. Crap like that doesn't happen here, you understand? Not on my watch." Tidwell nodded again. "Alright, I'm not saying we have a serial killer, but just in case, find out everything you can about those cases and see if there are any links. We have to nail this sick bastard before he kills again." The Sheriff turned to leave then stopped and spun around, again facing Tidwell. "Tell me what you need and it's yours. Understand? I want this guy." Aaron sat quietly not responding. "You're my man on this. Close it and you get the glory. Don't and well....," his voice faded off. "You know what I'm saying." Tidwell knew only too well.

The afternoon was spent canvassing those who knew the victims. By sundown Tidwell formulated a simplified portrait of the deceased. Friendly; but not buddy-buddy to anyone. Not unsocial but not out going. Adam was described as dependable and competent by his employer but not one to participate in water cooler gossip. Cordial in his dealings with others but stand-offish if he thought someone was trying to get to close. No one could remember him every discussing his off duty habits or interests. He didn't smoke, no one had ever seen him take a drink, although they were sure he did by his purchases of wine, and his name didn't appear in the membership of any church congregation. He had no credit cards, paying cash for all purchases. During his lifetime he accumulated no motor vehicle infractions and no criminal record.

Joyce worked part time in a day care. Attractive, beautiful to some, with long dark hair, green eyes, and a blemish free complexion she was described as likeable, good with children, but not really known. Like her husband she didn't engage in gossip. Although invited to the homes of co-workers the invitations were rebuffed with excuses. No invitations had been extended by her. She was known to have an occasional cigarette, a fact she attempted but failed to keep from the public. Only once, around the holidays, did she accompany her fellow day care workers for an after hours drink. She left after twenty minutes. Like her husband, Joyce's name never turned up on any police log or in traffic court.

Amanda had had blonde hair and blue eyes, a thin, well proportioned figure but was considered more attractive than Joyce. Her only blemish was a patch of red skin, a birth mark, on the back of her right leg which, when dressed in the short skirts she frequently wore during the summer, was clearly visible. An honor student, she was liked by her teachers but not by the other students. Snob was the one word which was most often used. Stand-offish with an attitude of superiority was one students quote. No after school activities, no clubs, no boy friends that anyone was aware of, no special girl friend to share lunch, or secrets, or girl talk.

The house in which they lived and died was a rental. When they moved in the deposits and six months advanced rent was paid up front in cash. Every month since, the rent was paid before it was due, always in cash, always with crisp new hundred dollar bills. Their computer was completely destroyed in the fire, along with any insight it might have contained of the family. If family pictures existed, they, as well as Adam's wallet and the females' purses were also completely destroyed.

What did survive the blaze was found on the second floor. An assortment of clothing, shoes, bath articles, six pistols found in the dresser drawers, a diary with no entries, and several intimate adult aids. In the detached garage were the two family vehicles. Both used when purchased. Both free of any clutter or clues. The victims were as mysterious and elusive as their assailant. It would be difficult to piece together a concrete narrative of their last hours.

Sitting on his desk when Tidwell returned to his office was a note to call Joe Sawyer. On the phone the SBI agent sounded exhausted. Having already been at work for fourteen hours Tidwell could empathize with him.

"We maybe stepping into something neither of us expected," Sawyer said.

"How's that?" Tidwell asked.

"The victims may not be related, not biologically anyway."

"Care to explain that?"

Sawyer sighed. "I've been on the phone most of the afternoon with Colorado and Arkansas. In both cases DNA proved the youngest victim was not the natural daughter of either of the adult victims. I think that's more than just coincidence. Don't be surprised if the same holds true here. "

"What are we talking about?" Tidwell ran his hands through his hair. "Are you saying both girls were adopted? That is a coincidence."

"Honestly I don't know," Sawyer replied. "That would be an easy explanation and make us feel like idiots or it could prove to be something sinister and prove we are idiots for not seeing it sooner."

"When will DNA be back on the victims?" Tidwell's tiredness crept into his voice.

"Another day or two at the best. Because of the circumstances we put a rush on everything. Our lab's working around the clock."

"What else can you tell me?" Aaron threw a cigar in his mouth.

"Not enough to solve this thing," Sawyer retorted. "but more than we knew yesterday. I'll be over to see you in the morning."

"Will I be happy to see you?" Tidwell stopped chewing the cigar while he waited for Sawyer's answer.

There was a long pause before the SBI agent responded. "I'm almost certain you won't be, but we'll talk about that tomorrow. I'll have Colorado's files in the morning. I'll see you after that."

CHAPTER FIVE

Built in 1914 atop a hill on the west side of Sylva, the Jackson County courthouse was situated to have a panoramic view down Main Street and its mixture of unique shops and cafes. To reach the courthouse from street level it would be necessary to ascend the picturesque and numerous steps. It had been widely reported that the courthouse was the most photographed courthouse in the state. By Tuesday morning its tranquility, and that of Sylva's, was transformed to a state of siege by the hordes of reporters representing the national media. The normally serene Township achieved instant notoriety.

The tip line was activated and instantly flooded with calls. Each one required extensive time and energy from an investigator. The SBI, claiming jurisdiction, assumed control of the case. Joe Sawyer was appointed lead and, after much heated conversations between state and county officials, Aaron Tidwell was temporarily assigned to Sawyer. As task force foot soldiers they were given a team of six investigators. Their command center, a makeshift grouping of rooms was hastily filled with desks, files, and phones and was located in the basement of the courthouse. They were granted the authority to request any necessary police assets and directed to call the Attorney General if those requests were ignored.

Scheduling a press conference for eleven, Joe Sawyer arrived from Asheville shortly before ten. In the tired and worn offices, surrounded by the members of his task force, he quickly established the chain of command. It was on their shoulders, he told everyone, that the task of solving this crime had fallen. The world was watching, not from afar, but from right outside the door. Failure would not only embarrass the state and the county, it would place all their reputations and careers in a less than favorable light.

At precisely eleven o'clock, accompanied by Tidwell, Sawyer walked up to the waiting microphone and faced the mob of reporters. "I have a brief statement," he said. "After which we will take questions for ten minutes and ten minutes only."

Removing a five by five index card from his jacket pocket he read. "Sometime between Saturday night and the early hours of Sunday morning, three people identified as Adam Cromwell, Joyce Cromwell, and Amanda Cromwell were murdered in their home off of Thomas Valley Ranch Road. At this time the investigation is ongoing and no additional details are available. The SBI with the assistance of the Jackson County Sheriff's office are working non-stop to apprehend the person or persons responsible for these murders. Thank you." He pointed to a reporter.

Identifying himself from ABC, the reporter asked, "Do you have any suspects?

"We are diligently working all leads as we get them." Sawyer answered before pointing to another reporter.

"Sylva Herald," the reporter identified himself. "The house where the murders were committed was burned. Can you tell us if the fire was an attempt to cover up the crime?"

"That's speculation." Sawyer replied crisply.

"Was this a random act or did the victims know their murderer?" someone yelled.

Sawyer took a deep breath before responding. "Our investigation is not at the stage where we can make that call."

The AP reporter spoke next. "It is rumored that the females were sexually assaulted. Can you confirm that or is it just a rumor?"

"The autopsies are not completed. Right now I can't confirm or deny anything. One more question, please. We have a lot of work to do."

"In the past four years there have been similar cases; one in Arkansas and one in Colorado. Do you know or do you suspect that this may be the work of the same killer?"

"What news agency do you represent?" Sawyer asked.

"The New York Times," answered the reporter.

"Let me say this. In the last four years there have been a substantial number of murders throughout the United States, not just Colorado and Arkansas." Sawyers tone turned colder. "Do me a favor and don't rush to judgments or print rumors or innuendos, it does no one any good. We are professionals who have been in the business for a number of years. I think between Detective Tidwell and myself we have close to forty-five years experience. Let us do our jobs and we'll let you do yours. Thank you." Turning his back on the cameras he left.

Back in the safety of their basement offices Sawyer retrieved a file from his desk and handed it to Tidwell. "Colorado," he said. Taking the thick manila file Tidwell settled into his chair. "Aaron," Sawyer said. "I just want you to know I'm not trying to steal your thunder.

You're a good cop. This whole task force thing wasn't my ideal. Like you I'm just following orders."

"Joe," Tidwell replied looking him in the eyes. "I have a feeling there's going to be plenty of heat from this thing to go around. I'm glad I'm not in the hot seat by myself."

The file contained over a hundred pages of typewritten interviews. The glossy pictures numbered forty. The autopsy report, toxicology reports, DNA reports, and police reports added another sixty pages. It would take time to interpret and understand the contents.

The pictures had an eerie similarity to the scene he'd seen on Sunday. Three bodies on one bed; the male bound to headboard and footboard and shot in the head, his blood spattered across the wall. The older female on her right side, eyes closed, head by the males feet. Close ups showed no bruising .The younger female on her back on the opposite side of the male, eyes open, legs spread apart with an artificial rose between them. Both females wore bright red lipstick. The room was sparsely furnished; bedding thrown in a heap on the floor. Clothes scattered. The windows, having no blinds or drapes, were bare.

The victims lived in the community for five years but were not well known. No close friends, no memberships, no bank accounts, no debts, a rented house in an isolated area, not easily seen from the road. The hair on the back of Tidwell's neck began to stand up. The lifestyles between the victims in Colorado and North Carolina were unnerving. A hard working but unsociable father, a mother who only worked part time, and a daughter who was a honor student but had no other activities outside of the home.

He read the autopsy report several times. The father died of a single gunshot wound to the head. The bullet, a twenty-two, penetrated the skull, exploding bone fragments which became projectiles, damaging the pros encephalon, which controls respiration. The injury, combined with blood loss induced death. If he had survived, the damage would have been severe enough he would have become a vegetable. The post mortem operation indicated over all good health. He had, at some point in his life, had a vasectomy. No traces of illegal drugs were discovered.

The females died of heart failure; the cause an abnormally high quantities of epinephrine. A naturally produced hormone in the human body, adrenaline as it is commonly called, is released in times of stress making the heart beat faster and opening veins for increased oxygen flow. Having more than the sufficient amount of epinephrine caused the hearts to beat faster than sustainable and they had, in layman's terms, worked themselves to death. The source of the excessive hormone was believed to have been from an injection. A single needle mark was found on the left arms of both.

Both females showed signs of definite sexual activity before death. Although there were no bruising or signs of forced trauma the external organs of their genitals, the labia major, the labia minor, and the clitoris were swollen from what could only be assumed was extended activity. Limited fluids were found inside the older female but were contaminated with a foreign substance and deemed unsuitable for testing. Toxicology revealed that foreign substance to be traces of bleach in both her vagina and her mouth. Bleach was also present in the mouth of the younger female. Usable fluids were however, recovered from her vagina. DNA results proved the fluids had the same makeup as the DNA of the male victim. The DNA comparison also proved the younger female was not the natural daughter of either of the older victims.

No other forensic evidence was recovered from the scene. With the exception of a partial print, the fingerprints were matched to the victims. A single photograph found in a bedroom drawer showed the victims in happier times by a swimming pool. Smiling for the camera they were posed in a group embrace. What separated it from any other photo that any family would take while on vacation was the fact that all three were naked. Their bodies went unclaimed. No next of kin could be located. A year after their deaths, the three were buried in unmarked graves.

The search of that home produced similar handguns as they found in the bedroom of the burnt Jackson County home. Similar aides for enhanced sexual pleasure were also noted on the inventory. Like the Cromwell's, the two family vehicles were late models and held no clues to the crime or insights into the lives of their owners.

"Something is wrong," Tidwell said to no one in particular.

Sawyer, looking up from his desk asked, "What?"

"The lack of evidence," Tidwell whispered. Clearing his throat he continued. "Now think about this, an unknown person or persons enters a home, has sexual contact with two females, and possibly the male victim as well and leaves no trace? And my guess is that it wasn't a bam-bam, thank you down and dirty, let me kill you and get out of here type of thing. I think it was slow, elaborated, no sense of urgency. And you want me to believe there was no transfer of hair in the genital areas, no transfer of body sweat? That doesn't make any sense."

"I told you this guy is as smart as us." Sawyer stood up rubbing his face with both hands. "There are a lot of questions I was hoping to have answered by reading those files. All it did was muddy the waters."

"We need to break this down into categories," Tidwell said standing up and crossing the room. On a dry eraser board he wrote, WHAT WE KNOW - WHAT WE THINK - and WHAT WE DON'T

KNOW. "Okay, let's do the easy one first. There are nine victims in three states. We know that - three men, three women, three girls. All the victims lived in semi-isolated locations in mountainous states. All the victims rented their homes. All the victims were quiet, unsociable people. All the victims had had sexual activity before death."

"What we don't know is easy," said Sawyer. He walked to the board and took the marker from Tidwell. "Who killed them? Why were they killed? Why were they targeted? What was the victim's relationship to each other? How did the killer cover his tracks? Where is the killer now?"

"Okay, what about what we think?" Tidwell queried.

"That should be discussed by the task force as a whole. What I think," Sawyer stated, "Is that we are stepping into a world in which we know very little - possible sexual exhibition, or sexual deviation, along with child molestation, and possible child pornography. It's a world normal people rarely come in contact with."

"What about the girls," Tidwell asked. "If they weren't the biological daughters, and I can't imagine a natural parent forcing their children into such acts of perversion, and we can't find any proof of adoption, where did they come from?"

"Hell if I know." Sawyer shook his head. Looking at his watch he realized he had been up for close to thirty hours. "We all need to get some rest," he said. "This thing is going to eat us alive. In the morning we'll be able to think better. Right now I need a drink and some sleep."

The phone rang. "Better put a hold on that," said Tidwell as he picked up the receiver. Listening intently he jotted a few notes on a legal pad. "Where is he now? ….. Right…..Got it…..Don't do anything." After hanging up he shook his head. "Every person in the county must know what we don't. Tip line brings all the weirdoes out of hiding. Don't these people have any better way to get their jollies?"

"What is it?" Sawyer asked, a smile creeping across his face.

"Patrol responded to a tip," answered Tidwell. "According to the caller our killer was walking down the expressway naked waving a gun around. Sure enough they picked up this fool walking naked beside the road. His gun was a cap pistol."

"Where is he now?" Sawyer asked his smile widening.

"Oh, they got him over at booking. He's drunk as a skunk. Disoriented," Tidwell said allowing himself a chuckle. "Anybody want to go talk to him? His name is Raymond Johnson. He lives over by Webster. They pick him up three, four times a year for public intoxication. First time he's been naked. Guess this mess got him excited. Anybody want to talk with him?" He looked around the room at the other detectives. Nobody answered. "Okay, I'll talk with him in the morning. God save me from a concerned public."

Taking the Colorado file with him Tidwell exited the building moving towards his vehicle. He would start reading the interviews after having dinner. As he unlocked his door a reporter called out his name.

"How can I help you?" Aaron said spinning to face whoever had spoken. The face of a disheveled reporter peered at him through the night's darkness.

"Detective, there's been a report that a nude male carrying a gun is in custody. Can you comment on that?"

The expression on Tidwell's face changed from tiredness to disgust. "For the love of God!" he exclaimed. "Get a life! Leave a poor old drunk alone." Getting in his car he slammed the door, started the engine, and sped away.

CHAPTER SIX

By Friday afternoon the reports from the autopsy were finished. In the pages of the report Task Force suspicions were confirmed. The similarities between these homicides and the others became sharper, clearer, but remained out of the realm of understanding. None of the crimes could be classified as random. Without argument these victims were targeted, their executions extensively planned and carried out. Yet the vagueness of why or how they were targeted remained as mysterious as the lives of the victims themselves.

In an attempt to learn more about the Cromwell's, Sawyer, through the efforts of the Attorney General, secured a warrant directing the mail of the victims to be delivered to the task force. Besides the overabundance of junk mail that appears in everyone's mail box there was little to shed light on who they'd been. Typical catalogues like *Plow and Hearth, Pottery Barn,* and, *L.L. Bean* filled their postal box. The most risqué of the mass mailings received was *Victoria's Secret,* a magazine that could be found in a large percentage of the nation's homes.

"I still think the key is the girls," Tidwell said, speaking to all the members of the task force. "None were the offspring and none were related biologically to the older victims. Solve that question and you've taken a giant leap into solving all three crimes."

"Did anyone check to see if the girls were related to each other?" one of the detectives asked. "That could be what ties all of it together."

"That's a thought," said Sawyer. "I'll have the lab do a comparison." He picked up the phone and punched in the numbers to the lab.

The basement offices had been transformed from the typical to those resembling a war room. On the walls the glossy pictures of each victim hung like prized art work. Anyone walking into the office would instantly be greeted by the grizzly photos. Beneath and beside the pictures pages torn from yellow legal pads were taped. Printed in black magic marker were the known facts about each victim. Printed in red magic marker were the facts still unknown. On an easel sized piece of paper the words TIME LINE were printed. Working on the principle of backward planning, the only time written at the bottom of the paper was the time the fire was reported.

The files from Colorado and Arkansas had been housed in a separate file cabinet. The files they were accumulating in their own investigation quickly spilled from one cabinet to a second. Each hot line call was being followed up, an interview done with the caller, a report completed, and a file began. For every interview and report accomplished and filed, there remained ten to do.

"Let's do this." Tidwell swung around and faced the photos. "I know it's a long shot that's going to require a lot of resources and man hours, but maybe we'll get lucky."

"What is it?" Sawyer asked as he hung up the phone.

"I'm just thinking out loud here guys. Have DMV give us a report of names and address of everyone they have issued a driver's license to in the past two years. Have Colorado give us the same report for the two years which preceded that and Arkansas a report for the two years preceding that."

"Christ, Tidwell," a detective said. "That will be thousands and thousands of names."

"Compare the lists and see if any name comes up on all three." Tidwell shook his head. "I know it's a long shot. The guy might not even be using the same name. But if he feels safe why would he change it? That might be his screw up."

"This isn't T. V. with super powered computers. Doing that could take months - maybe longer. The man may not even live in North Carolina. You know the state line isn't very far away. And you're going on the assumption that he has a license." Chet Springs, a ten year veteran of SBI, said. He dropped his reading glasses on his desk, looking at Tidwell. "How much time do you think we have?"

"Two years," Tidwell replied. "If nothing sets him off and he holds to his pattern, we have two years." He took his seat at his desk. "Look guys, I know we all want to catch this son-of-a-bitch as soon as we can. But before we can catch him we have to identify him and short of him walking in and confessing, that's what's going to take the time, and the work, and the manpower. Hell, if we knew who he was we could just go out and arrest him, or shoot him, I really don't care which, and then we'd all go home. But we can't do either until we know his name."

Sawyer reluctantly agreed. "I'll ask for the reports. When we get them I'll see if I can get a little more manpower to help us."

The office door opened interrupting their discussion. A uniformed deputy carried in the day's mail for the Cromwell's. "There's a lady outside who would like to see one of you," the deputy stated. "She says she has information you will be interested in."

"Did she ask for anyone in particular?" Sawyer wanted to know.

The deputy shook his head. "Okay." He turned to Tidwell. "Aaron, you and Chet want to handle her? I'll go through the mail."

"No problem," Tidwell said picking up a legal pad from the desk. Springs followed him out the door.

In its past history the room was referred to as the gray room. Used for more practical purposes, it was center stage for counting the historic ballots of 1913 in which the seat of government had been wrestled from Webster and granted to Sylva. Since those glory days it had been reduced to the storage of boxed files and dust collecting furniture. Adjoining the basement offices of the task force the need for the room, for however temporary, was resurrected.

Furnished with a single walnut table in the center, the room's seating accommodations consisted of three wooden chairs in desperate need of refinishing. The room was bland, lacking distinction. The brick walls original color and beauty had, though the years, been buried under uncountable coats of numerous colors of paint. The last application transformed the walls to a battleship gray. From the ceiling, directly over the table, hung a shadeless incandescent light. The starkness of the high wattage bulb compounded the inhospitable atmosphere.

Entering the room Tidwell and Springs found a short, middle aged brown haired woman waiting. She stood when she saw them. "I'm Detective Tidwell with the Jackson County Sheriff's office, and," pointing to Springs, "This is Detective Springs from the SBI. Please have a seat,"

All three sat down. The chairs were positioned so the questioners would be opposite those that were being questioned. "What is your name?" Springs asked.

"Debra Isdell." She smiled as she spoke.

"And were do you live Mrs. Isdell?" Tidwell asked, returning her smile.

"Thomas Valley Ranch Road." The detectives looked at one another.

"How can we help you?" Springs inquired as Tidwell wrote on the legal pad.

"Well, I think it is I who can help you. I think I know who did those awful things."

"And what awful things might you be referring to? Tidwell asked as he stopped writing and looked directly in her eyes.

"Those awful murders of course." Placing a hand at the base of her neck she continued. "I am certain I saw the lunatic who killed those poor people."

Springs sat back in his chair studying the face of Debra Isdell. Finally he asked, "When did you see him and what exactly did you see?"

"Last Sunday morning I had to take my dog out so he could do his business, you know. I always walk him close to the road. I am not very good with directions and such so I always make sure I know how to get home. Anyway, there he was, driving like a wild man down the road, with no lights on, can you believe it?"

"What time was that?" Tidwell wanted to know.

"I'm not sure. It could have been around two, maybe a little later."

"And the kind of a car he was driving, Mrs. Isdell," Springs pressed. "Can you remember what kind of car it was? Old, young - maybe what color?"

"Again, I can't really say. It was dark you know and, well; I'm not really good at telling one car from another. All those foreign cars they all look alike to me."

Springs leaned in and crossed his arms on the table. "Did you get a look at the license plate?"

"As I say it was dark."

"That's okay Mrs. Isdell," Tidwell comforted her. "You're doing fine. Can you describe the man in the car?"

"I don't think so. As I told you a couple of times it was dark and, well, I was trying to get out of the way. And I was trying to keep my dog out of the way. If anything happened to him my husband would kill me."

After several more questions they reviewed with Mrs. Isdell what she had told them. Prodding, coaching, soothing, reassuring, Tidwell and Springs extracted whatever information she believed she possessed. "I guess I wasn't much help after all," she said.

Thanking her for coming in both detectives walked her out then returned to the task force room.

"Anything good?" Sawyer asked as they entered.

"Not enough," replied Tidwell. In a condensed version he related the interview. Still, he added the scant information to the time line.

"We have something, but I'm not sure what." Sawyer said picking up an envelope up from his desk. "It came in today's mail for the Cromwell's." He handed it to Tidwell. "We've had it dusted for prints. There are plenty but probably none usable."

The envelope's postmark was Hamburg, Germany. There was no return address. Inside was a nondescript single sheet of paper used in nearly every household printer. Tracing its origin would be difficult if not impossible. Unfolding the page he read the text:

Cromwell's

Thank you for the tapes you sent us. We really liked watching them. We have watched them many times and each time it is better and more exciting. It is wonderful to live as you do. My English is not good enough to say how we feel. We are sending you some of our pictures and a recording. We ask if this is alright to do.

It is not always that you find people the same as you are and are not afraid. Please write with questions.

Thank you.

Hans Griener

Tidwell looked at Springs and then at Sawyer. "What is this all about?"

"I don't know." Sawyer said. "But I don't think we are going to like it. We'll send it to the lab and ask Hamburg to see if they can locate this guy. See if he has any insight into our victims."

"Clues to what happened to them would be better." Springs said. "Everyday we get sucked deeper and deeper into a tar pit and it's starting to boil."

"What are you telling me here?" asked Tidwell. "That the Cromwell's belonged to some perverse sex circles were people swap partners and kids?" He looked around the room. "I know it goes on but did something happen and Jackson County get sent into the twilight zone? If it did they forgot to tell me."

"Hard to say," answered Sawyer. "It could be. There's a whole world out there that the guy down the street hasn't got a clue about. But that's a good thing. That world is not pretty."

CHAPTER SEVEN

In his dream he was suspended above the room, floating effortlessly, able to see but invisible to other eyes. Consumed by their own passions the participants on the bed were ignorant of his presence. The irony of his invisibility made him laugh knowing the loudness of his laughter would fall silently on their ears. His eyes absorbed their movements; like a camera captures images; his eyes retained and filed every second of the union. Prior to achieving their unleashed desires a third person entered the room and temporarily interrupted them.

The intruder had long hair the color of midnight, sulking lips, and a flawless complexion. The full length gown she wore shielded the extent of her natural beauty. Slowly she crossed the room. Standing beside the bed she allowed the gown to slide from her shoulders revealing her body. With the robe pooled at her feet she stepped onto the bed, her arms encircling those already there. Stroking, touching, kissing, she fanned the flames of their passion, urging them to fulfillment. With the rasping sounds of approaching satisfaction filling the room she turned and glared upward toward him. Minutes ticked by. His ears pounded from the increasing sounds of pleasure. His eyes were frozen on her face. Never had he viewed such flawless perfection. He was aroused and he inched closer to the trio in an attempt to touch them. He ached with his desire. Suddenly her head fell backwards and her mouth, spewing the laugh of the dead, opened wide. Looking into the darkness of her gaping mouth he saw the souls of the damned, saw their evil and behind them the flames of Hell.

He awoke with a jolt, covered in sweat. Throwing the bed covers off he swung his feet to the floor and sat up. Shaking his head he stood then made his way to the kitchen sink where he splashed cold water on his face. Toweling off he sat in the darkness of the living room smoking a cigarette.

Born to a mother unable to fend for herself, much less an infant, at the age of two he was shuttled off to live with two unmarried aunts. Although financially capable of providing for their new responsibility, their existence, permissiveness and lack of a structured regimen, would, in most households, be problematic. For their impressionable young ward, the progressiveness of their lifestyle was disastrous. By the time he was ten he could no longer be classified as normal. The rare punishments for misconduct were atypical, their lessons unforgettable, the transgressions which caused them never repeated.

Naturalists and uninhibited, the sisters habitually shed their clothing as soon as they were safely in the privacy of the home. Interior doors had no locks and were never shut. Meals were prepared and consumed in the nude. Except on rare occasions meant to impress community leaders with their clothed graciousness, those individuals invited into the sanctuary of the home were people of the same mindset. With the fear of being mocked at school, the circumstances in the home precluded him from extending invitations to classmates or acquaintances.

The physiological abuse began when he entered the home. The sexual abuse began when he was in the seventh grade. Long accustomed to the nudity he succumbed to his surroundings, shedding his clothes once inside the front door. At first he didn't realize it was abuse. There was an occasional bumping against his bare buttocks or a hand lingering on his chest accidentally. All innocent he assumed. Soaking in the bathtub one evening he was surprised by the appearance of one Aunt offering her assistance to help him bathe. Reluctantly agreeing to her wishes he endured the over attentiveness she bestowed in the area of his genitals.

Finally there was no more pretending.

After a night when his aunts freely poured glasses of wine, of which he had also partaken, they retreated to the bedroom they shared and sent him to his. Asleep for a short period of time he sensed more than felt the hand between his legs. At first, thinking the hand was his he responded to its movement. Once fully awake he realized his hands were by his side and the knowledge made him afraid to open his eyes. It was safer, he thought, to pretend nothing was happening and he forced his mind to find another world where everything and everybody was happy. Afterwards he lay quiet, hardly breathing, and unsure of what would happen. Thinking it was only a nightmare he was sure he would wakeup. Embarrassment mixed with his confusion. Ashamed he actually enjoyed the unwanted stimulation, he felt isolated, powerless to control his situation. The feeling disgusted him.

The frequency gradually escalated. The rituals became almost nightly, until finally, in a measure of self-preservation and anger he capitulated, becoming a willing partner in the incestuous relationships. His willingness made him bolder. Their roles changed. No longer satisfied to being the abused he progressed to being the abuser, forcing them to act out his every fantasy.

Dropping out of school as soon as he was legally able he moved out of the home and headed west. Unemployed with no income he survived on the streets by panhandling and shoplifting. Famished and stranded in Nevada, he met a woman who took pity on him. Taking him into her home she provided the outlet he needed to regain his strength.

During the days she fussed over him, made him accomplish chores around the house, bought him clothes, and taught him to drive. At night, leaving him on his own, she would go to work in a local brothel. Her profession did not bother him. Her absences provided him the time necessary to explore and then refine his obsessions.

Their relationship eventually turned intimate. It ended in anger and rage when she objected to the continual addition of someone younger and younger to their sexual marathons. By that time he was full gown with powerful hands. He had little trouble silencing her. The feeling of power and invincibility that roared through his body as she jerked in the throes of death exhilarated him. Never had he felt such peacefulness. Loading her into the trunk of her car he drove into the desert. Knowing the coyotes would soon feast on her carcass he buried her in a shallow grave. Unable to return to the house he pointed the car towards California, stopping in Los Angles. Abandoning the car at a bus stop and wiping it clean of prints, he melted into the streets.

To him, the Los Angles underworld was enthralling - drugs, prostitution, gambling, and secret clubs where any fantasy could become reality. With his size and strength and his willingness to blur the lines of legality he had no problem securing employment. But it wasn't the money that interested him. Money was the means to satisfy his needs. In the world in which he moved and lived, opportunity for self gratification was more essential than money. The longer he stayed, the deeper he sunk into his perversions. His quest for the ultimate satisfaction eluded him. His sessions of sex evolved from reality to macabre. Proclaiming himself a disciple he viewed himself as the teacher of the uneducated and the path to salvation for those less enlightened. He found few whose orientation mirrored his. If he did stumble upon them he clung to them in a suffocating way. His realization of their lack of commitment to his idealized paradise sent him into fits of uncontrollable anger and left him feeling empty and drained.

Unexpectedly he stumbled across a society he originally thought was a myth; a small clandestine society living the lifestyle and sexual freedom which he preached. Doubting the validity of such rumors, yet praying for the gossips reality, he began his research. But the research required skill, cunning, and absolute dedication. Through contacts he made during his years of living in Los Angles' seedy districts he made cautious inquiries. Most were answered with blank stares or laughter. On many occasions he was told he was dreaming. Persistence, and intermittent physical incentives to aid those whose mental recall was deficient, at last paid off. Uncovering the well hidden organization was his triumph. Unlocking the door which would allow him entrance to his perceived earthly paradise was his humiliation.

Cults are, by necessity, secretive in nature. Historically they have also been notorious for their propensity towards mental control of their members. For cults brainwashing is commonly referred to as education or indoctrination. The secret society upon which he stumbled was not immune to those loathsome traits. Much like other cults it had been founded on illogical beliefs and built on foundations which extracted, then distorted biblical passages and laws of nature.

Founded on the mysticism of monogamy being in opposition to the laws of nature, the society advocated sexual intimacy with multiple partners. The age requirement of acceptable partners was not restrictive. Quoting Bible references to plural partners and embracing the position of fundamentalist members of the Mormon faith who continue polygamous marriages, members proclaimed themselves free of prejudices. Freed of inhibitions, after indoctrination, they attempt to fashion their lives on their teachings. Remaining under the radar of local officials was a prerequisite. Existing purely for the sexual pleasures of its members, the society, whose ranks contained well educated and highly literate people, knew the discovery of the activities would result in extensive prison sentences.

The flaw in their reasoning was the children. Unlike the fundamentalists who had had decades to parent their future generations, the society required immediate injection of acceptable and willing minor females. The very lucrative trade of human trafficking, combined with the necessary program of indoctrinations, eliminated that shortage.

Locations of meetings were held in the strictest of confidentiality and with good cause. Only at these meetings were society members allowed to socialize with those outside their family units. Billed as forums for discussions on problem solving, living undetected, and maintaining the impression of respectability in the communities, the meetings ultimately disintegrated into a spring board for the continuation of self-gratification. Resembling the private clubs dedicated to emotionless copulation the so named conventions were nothing more than an opportunity to participate in organized orgies.

But his discovery of the forbidden fruit failed to guarantee him permission to partake. Membership was maintained and extended through cautious internal conversations, rigid investigations, and unanimous recommendations. Self enrollment was an impossibility. To the average person rejected membership would be a disappointing bump in the road. Although possibly upset, the ill feelings would, over the course of time, fade away.

He was not the average person. Mental illness, in the truest sense normally strikes individuals in their prime, usually during adolescence or young adulthood. His history and experiences of abuse at the hands of family members had rearranged what would be considered a logical thought process. Engaged in distorted thinking, it was simple for him to rationalize and justify his behavior. From his failure to gain an invitation to a meeting the seed of vengeance was planted. By the time the seed bloomed it was cultivated into an obsession.

Meeting the girl in Colorado was accidental. Beautiful, young, uneducated, and impressionable with an eagerness to fulfill his fantasizes, she had, for awhile derailed his search for those who denied him. Like their daughter, the backwoods parents were easily influenced. Pitting his sophisticated knowledge of the world against their naive understanding of what he truly wanted made the process even easier. Allowing a period of time to pass and with the promise of a better life, he carted her away and resumed his quest. Her youth enabled him to mold her attitude, to shape her understanding and comprehension of relationships; to accept his reasoning as to the necessity of multiple couplings. At first tentative, she reluctantly conceded to the three person trysts he arranged. Ashamed to admit openly she enjoyed the experiences she allowed him to believe she participated solely for his pleasure. For him it was living his own version of the society.

In the mountains of Arkansas he uncovered the first society family. Stealing what time he could from his duties at work and duties at home he began his surveillance. In the weeks that followed he became an expert on their activities. Knowing their locations at any given time provided him the luxury of free rein inside their home, where he acquired additional information on them and discovered hidden society material. The pictures and videos he found aroused him but not as much as finding the names and address of other members. Leaving no trace of his intrusion there was no reason for them to suspect an invasion of their privacy. Once their re-education was completed he would salvage the material to use as a roadmap to others

Every second was planned and rehearsed. Every detail thought out, refined, and perfected. There was, he knew, no second chance. Command was his from the time he entered the dark house. "No turning back," he said to himself. The expectation of what was to happen electrified his body. His face, flush with desire, illuminated his being. Never did he tremble. At all times he was calm and cool. His voice was controlled. His movements were graceful. His eyes twinkled with joy.

Unhurried, he was there for three hours. With the unlimited time he explored every conceivable degradation, growing bolder with each command. Their compliance only served to fuel his fantasizes compelling new instructions. So quick they had been to obey. So eager were they to gain his approval. Then it was over.

Standing over the bed looking down at the bodies he sighed. Bending over he gently kissed their faces. Not since the killing in Nevada had he felt so satiated. After positioning the bodies how he wanted them and placing the rose between the girl's legs he packed his things not forgetting to claim his trophies.

Outside the crispness of the night air did little to cool the heat of his body. Driving away he smoked a cigarette, turned the radio to where he could just barely hear the music, and relived the past few hours in his mind. Crawling into bed he slept like a baby

Her voice startled him from his reverie and he unconsciously jumped. "What?" he asked.

"Are you alright?" she repeated. Realizing he was no longer in bed she had gone in search of him.

"Alright?" The question startled him. "Yes, yes. Everything is fine. I was just sitting here thinking." He lit another cigarette, inhaling deeply. When he exhaled the thin smoke filtered up towards her face forming a crude frame of her features.

"It's almost dawn," she told him. "If we are going to Knoxville today you should come back to bed and get some sleep."

"Your right," he whispered. "I'll be along shortly." Turning away she left him alone with his thoughts. Crushing out the half finished cigarette he returned to the bedroom. Everything is fine, he said to himself. Everything would always be fine.

CHAPTER EIGHT

Summer in Jackson County, North Carolina is picturesque, its scenery proudly displayed on the front of thousands of post cards. The days are splashed with the warmth of perfection while the nights offer idyllic temperatures. A major tourist attraction, the area's diversity offers something for everyone. The Tuckasegee River, beginning at the confluence of Panthertown and Greenland creeks and flowing in a northwesterly direction before dumping into the Tennessee River in Swain County, is named for a tribe of the Cherokee nation. Its waters are home to brook, rainbow, and brown trout. Their bountiful numbers lure many fishermen to pass countless hours along the river banks, their serenity disrupted only by those in need of the excitement of rafting.

For nature lovers there are hiking trails. For golfers, more than challenging courses to test their skills. The Indian reservation offers cultural experiences. Their casino offers the chance to win big or lose big. The Great Smoky Mountain Railroad provides sightseeing excursions during the day and a dinner train at nights. And on the last Friday night of each month the county plays host to Friday Night Live, a showcase for the locally best of the best in folk, rock, country, bluegrass, and easy listening music. It is effortlessly easy to understand why the area is popular. For Aaron Tidwell, Joe Sawyer, and Chet Springs the summer months were no more enjoyable than those of the winter or spring.

With little development in the case and no suspect they could scrutinize, the hordes of national media no longer broadcast from the courthouse steps. The local papers now relegated their sporadic stories to page six instead of page one. The task force, attacked by everyone for their lack of progress and the amount of money needed to fund them suffered the slow demise through reassignment of its members. The fact that they had always been under budgeted and undermanned did nothing to quell public sentiment of incompetence. Only Sawyer, Springs, and Tidwell were allowed to remain. In a society which demands instant results, their lack of any results only boosted the publics' unfavorable perception.

Leads from the hot line, after the initial onslaught of nearly twelve hundred, evaporated. The line was terminated. Officials agreed that hysteria, not public service, was responsible for most of the calls received. Only the television show *America's Most Wanted,* through three separate segments, kept the story alive with pleadings for assistance from anyone who believed they held information relevant to the case. The three detectives knew what every cop knew. Often without additional crimes being committed and the possibility of gaining new leads from them, their odds of securing justice were reducing drastically fast. As summer twisted its way towards fall the three men's activities were reduced to the mundane. No self-respecting reporter was interested in a non-story. It was no surprise the multitude of reporters vanished.

In Hamburg, Hans Griener had been questioned and briefly detained by the German authorities. The search of his house was fruitless. The video of the Cromwell's, if one indeed existed, had either been destroyed or passed on to another viewer. Other than alerting possible associates that police scrutiny had begun, the Germany lead ran into a stone wall. Left with nothing of any substance the three man task force was reduced to the tedious examination of the available reports.

Repeated review of typed reports and photographs can, and does, often blur the vision of those processing the information. Criminal investigations have a capacity for the gathering of huge amounts of paperwork. The paperwork associated with a homicide investigation is enormous. Expanding those files were the files from two other investigations from two different states. Becoming proficiently familiar with all three was a monumental task. Still, they remained determined they would unravel the mystery. Their confidence, however, was not free of moments of doubt. Dependent on one another to foster their own morale, the trio's friendship deepened.

To sustain his resolve, Tidwell established a routine. Every night after the long hours of painstakingly reviewing files and re-interviewing those who contacted the tip line, he drove to the charred remains of the Cromwell's home. On some nights he would sit in his car and stare at the darkened structure. On others he would enter the building, climb the stairs, and stand in the bedroom where the bodies had been discovered. Desperately he endeavored to gain insight into the events of that horrific night. Sixty minutes would pass while he was locked in his thoughts trying to imagine the actions of the killer and the reaction of the victims. Long after his mind fatigued and his body was slumped with tiredness, he would start his car and make his way home.

"I've got him!" Springs shouted jumping from his chair in his excitement.

"Got who?" Tidwell asked looking up from pouring over the DMV reports of three states. Breaking the reports down alphabetically each man had taken a third of the alphabet.

"I've got the bastard! The killer!" Springs' voice flushed with his certainty.

"Yeah right," Tidwell responded with cynicism.

"Look! Arkansas, Colorado, North Carolina. All issued a drivers license within the two year period before the murders; all to the same man." Tidwell got up from his desk. "You were right Aaron," Chet said. "The DMV reports were the key. Jesus Christ! I'm staring at the man's name."

"Well," Tidwell said. "What's his name?"

"Lester. David Allen Lester. He has an address in Bryson City. DMV issued the license twenty months ago."

Tidwell remained skeptical. "Are you sure it is the same man and not three different guys with the same name?"

"Same last name, same first name, and same middle name. What are the chances three guys share all three names?" Springs looked at the reports spread across his desk. "And here's the clincher. They all have the same birth date."

"Walks like a duck," Tidwell said.

"Then it must be a duck." Springs finished the thought.

"Alright, I'll call Sawyer. But just to be on the safe side get a photo from all three states." Tidwell picked up the phone and punched in the numbers for Sawyer. "You know it might be just a fluke. He may not be our man. Let's find out everything we can about him. Start with the county records. Does he own his home or does he rent? If he rents who is his landlord? He is married or single? What does he do for a living? Did his path ever cross those of the victims? I don't want to spook him and I don't want him to know we know his name."

Sawyer had been called to Asheville for what was becoming a weekly homage to his superiors. Taking Tidwell's call, his heart started to race. Sweaty moisture covered his face. Saying only that they had uncovered a new lead which required his immediate attention, he begged forgiveness and started back towards Sylva. With the use of his flashing blue lights to break speed limits he drastically reduced the commuting time. Back in his office staring at Tidwell and Springs he had one question. "Are you sure?"

"Not a hundred percent," Tidwell replied. "But I think we may be getting close."

"One hundred percent," Sawyer said removing his jacket and loosening his tie. "That's what we have to be! One hundred percent! No reasonable doubt. No ifs, ands, or buts. We don't want to have spent nine months on this just to fail."

"We know he was in all three states," Tidwell clarified. "Maybe he's our guy, maybe not. Maybe it's three different guys with the same name. We don't know for sure yet. We've asked for pictures from DMV. But right now he is all we have to go on."

"Alright - alright. Go slowly. If he's our man even the smell of a cop snooping around will make him run. Damn! Can it be that easy?" Sawyer slapped Springs on the back. "Good work."

After two weeks another chart was added to the wall. At the top in capital letters they wrote the initials D. A. L. Beneath them were written what the detectives learned about their number one suspect.

Forty. No facial hair. No eyebrows. Bald or shaved? Handyman. Married? A question mark was placed beside the comment. Through surveillance they knew he was living with a younger woman but could find no record of a marriage license. No children. Renter not owner. Two vehicles. Attends church. No credit cards. No bank loans. No known friends. Home at night. Out of town travel once a month with wife. Beside that entry they wrote - where does he go? They also noted his behavior was surprisingly similar to that of the victims.

The chart prompted discussions. Sawyer, who had previously educated the task force on serial killers, seized the opportunity to expound on the subject. Quickly he entered into a litany of the origin of the word, the distinctiveness of the individuals, their psychology and development, and the two types - nonsocial offenders and asocial offenders - which the FBI generally categorize all serial killers.

Using strictly the clinical definition, this killer would fall into the former. An above average IQ, methodical planning, a more than average knowledge of forensic science, and socially adequate, also called the mask of sanity. More common than not is the killer's intense following of the media coverage. Newspaper clippings saved for prosperity. Scrap books devotedly maintained. Eluding and baffling the authorities enhances their feeling of power.

As Sawyer spoke he assumed the role of mentor, instructing the wards in his care. Slowly and patiently he reviewed the history of serial killers noting that the term, defined as the killing of three or more persons with a cooling off period between, did not appear until the 1970s, purportedly coined by an FBI agent. Briefly he spoke of the "MacDonald triad" which are possible warning signs and exhibited by some serial killers during childhood. The signs, fire starting for gaining attention or thrills, cruelty to animals for self enjoyment, and bed wetting beyond the age a child would normally grow out of the behavior, are not all inclusive and are no guarantee that those who exhibit the signs will become serial killers in adulthood. Hypotheses differ but a popular and widely accepted one is that all serial killers suffer from antisocial personality disorder. Usually not psychotic, they are able to function and mingle unnoticed in society to the extent of having spouses and children. Albert DeSalvo, the supposed Boston Strangler, and Dennis Rader, Wichita's BTK killer, were examples Sawyer used to emphasis his point.

His knowledge of the history of serial killers was impressive and he highlighted the names of Liu Pengli of China, a cousin of the Han Emperor Jing. Pengli murdered a hundred or more. Gilles de Rais, one of France's wealthiest men in the fifteenth century is believed to have abducted, raped, and murdered a hundred young boys who had come to his castle as pages. Elizabeth Bathory, the Hungarian aristocrat was arrested for the torture and butchering of six hundred young girls. Naturally he spoke of the world's most famous serial killer, Jack the Ripper who preyed on prostitutes, and whose actual body count, as well as his true identity, remains unknown. But most famous did not mean most prolific. That distinction belongs to Thug Behram, a gang leader of the Indian Thuggee cult of assassins who is reported to have strangled more than nine hundred victims using a ceremonial rumal. The cult as a whole is credited by the Guinness World Records with the murders of two million. Their infamy introduced the word thugs into English colloquial speech. When he was finished the three sat in silence.

Finally Springs spoke. "I want to bring him in for a sit down."

"You won't get anything," Sawyer countered. "You won't get anything."

"Search his house," Springs said pleading, his frustrations evident in his voice.

"Where's your probable cause?" Sawyer replied.

"It doesn't exist, that's where it is." Tidwell leaned back in his chair clasping his hands behind his head. "We don't even have a traffic ticket on this guy. We've been watching him for awhile now - nothing out of the ordinary. Hell. What judge are you going to get to issue a search warrant for ordinary? All we have is motor vehicle pictures. That doesn't constitute probable cause."

"There is something about him though," Sawyer said. "I can't put my finger on it but its there. You know what I mean? This guy is almost too perfect, too law abiding."

"Colorado and Arkansas have dug into him too. They've had about as much luck as we've had." Tidwell looked at his watch then rubbed his eyes. "You boys know that if we spook him we lose him. If we arrest him, the case gets thrown out for lack of evidence or worse it goes to trail and he gets acquitted for lack of evidence. Either way we lose him." He sighed heavily. "I'm with you. I think he's a person of interest but until we have something a little more conclusive we better walk a tightrope."

Springs cursed. "We can ask him to come in for a sit down," he said. "Under the guise of doing background on the Cromwell's. Perfectly legal."

Sawyer yawned, stood up, and rubbed his back. "Look. We can do that and then what? I'm just as frustrated as any of you but we can't let our emotions control our decisions."

"Then what do we do?" Springs demanded. His voice rising slightly.

"Watch him. Continue with what we are doing. Investigate him. We're cops. That's what we do and despite what people think I know we are pretty good at it.

Somewhere along the lines he will screw up. The bad guys always do."

"And if he doesn't?" Tidwell asked.

Sawyer's face was etched with fatigue. "If he doesn't - then he's not our man."

"Maybe we should take a trip. Check out Colorado and Arkansas ourselves." Tidwell remarked smiling. "I could use a vacation."

"Not a bad thought. No budget for it though." Sawyer thought for several moments. Starting to speak he stopped, retreating back into his thoughts. Carefully he weighed the possibilities of positive accomplishment against the probabilities of negative results. When he spoke again he reversed himself. "Guys, I'm tired. After nine months we've got nothing. Maybe Springs is right; maybe we need to force the issue. We ask Mr. Lester very politely to come in and have a sit down with us. There is no law against talking to people and it can't be construed as harassment. The DMV photos give us probable cause to do that much. Take the weekend. Spend time with your families. Bring him in for a face to face on Monday."

"And what are you going to do?" Springs asked Sawyer.

"Explain our actions to the Attorney General and see if I can get some rest. I haven't been feeling too well. And maybe a drink or two," he said with a laugh.

CHAPTER NINE

Forty miles east of Jackson County lay the city of Asheville, the seat of government for Buncombe County. Nestled in the Blue Ridge Mountains and, until 1793 named Morristown, Asheville was built on a high piece of ground where two Indian trails intersected. In its early days notable guests included such celebrities as Daniel Boone and Davy Crockett. Nothing more than a crude outpost, Asheville did not grow until the railroad arrived in 1880. Even then its growth was slow and meager. Black Friday and the following Great Depression hit the city hard. Nonetheless, Asheville remained and instead of defaulting on the municipal bonds it sold, the city, over a period of fifty years paid them off. Truly the city is a demonstration of determination and resilience.

Today the city is a mixture of architectural legacy and art, from art deco to beaux art to neo classical. George W. Vanderbilt's famous Biltmore Estate, the country's largest single family home, attracts a million plus visitors every year, as does the diverse mixture of art galleries and shops which line the sidewalks. October fall foliage is breathtaking as one drives along the Blue Ridge Parkway. But the long past rustic beginnings have not been forgotten and through historical preservation the past is celebrated and enjoyed.

The modern metropolitan area ranks high on the list as one of the best places to live in America. Indeed, some of the city's past residents have included such notables as F. Scott Fitzgerald and his wife Zelda who tragically died in a local mental institution during a fire. Robert Morgan, the man who piloted the famous World War II B17 bomber, The Memphis Belle, also made Ashville his home.

As with any large and sprawling modern city, Asheville also has its elements of a less than desirable character. Some came to reinvent themselves. Some came to hide from their pasts. Others migrated to the area for the seclusion of the numerous mountaintop homes and the privacy those sites offered. Behind the exterior walls and doors lay the freedom to indulge themselves in conduct, although not necessarily illegal, others would find culpable. It was to just such a home on the eastern outskirts of the city that he brought her.

The owner was a vibrant, thirty something, with shoulder length blonde hair, soft blue eyes, and thin lips. She greeted them with open arms and a flurry of kisses. The house was small in square footage but large in details. Stone countertops and handmade wood cabinets highlighted the modern stainless steel appliances and granite floors. Crown molding, painted in bold colors, separated ceilings from walls. A floor to ceiling stone fireplace dominated an entire wall in the great room. He remarked on the beauty of the home while thinking it was all ostentatious. They had not driven from their home to be impressed by material triumph. They had driven from their home to indulge themselves in basic, animalistic pleasures. Suffering through the necessary cordial, but meaningless, conversation he allowed his mind to envision what was about to transpire. Finally, the necessities complete, he ordered them to adjourn to the bedroom where he would follow momentarily.

Standing in the middle of the room he smoked a cigarette, taking his time and flicking the ashes in the fireplace. He had feasted his eyes on her scantily clothed figure, the sheer fabric failing to hide the movement of her breasts as she guided them through the house. The silk garment molded itself around her thighs leaving little to the imagination. Her beauty was not classic but a combination of exercise and skillful application of makeup. Despite her height she teetered on chubbiness, avoiding it solely through her physical exertions. Still, she aroused him and he bristled with expectancy.

Finished he tossed the butt onto the stone hearth and made his way towards the open bedroom door. When he entered the room the two women were nude on the bed. For a period of time he stood there watching their actions, snapping photographs. Caressing, fondling, exploring, they were oblivious to his presence. After disrobing by the door he spoke. "Now it's time to have some fun." Muffled giggles answered his voice. Climbing onto the bed he quickly became entangled between the two of them. Fantasy was replaced with reality. Integrated between the two women he conjured forth every craving he could conceive. Acting as a maestro he orchestrated the frenzied movements of the bed's occupants. Fending off fatigue he repeatedly staged the positions and supervised the actions of his collaborators. As fleeting as he knew it would be, for the moment he was as happy as he knew he could ever hope to be.

Driving back to Jackson County it began to rain and the slap of the wipers was the only audible sound within the car. She sat next to the passenger's door in silence. Behind the wheel, navigating the highway, he was inattentive to her. He preferred it that way. After their encounters she was habitually quiet. The first few times it happened he had questioned the silence. Attempting to analyze her withdraw cheated him from his own thoughts and the distraction angered him. Knowing the eventual out come would be awkward normalcy he blocked his mind to her antics. Now he did nothing to draw out her thoughts. He had no doubt that she took pleasure in their activities. Her moans and throaty emissions were obvious testaments to her pleasure. Her retreat into a hiatus from conversation was now familiar. No matter, he thought. The quietness provided his indulgence of the decadent memories.

The trip home was uneventful and as they pulled into their yard the rain settled into a fine mist. Inside, not bothering to turn on any lights they shed their clothing and slipped under the covers of the bed. Still flush with the night's passion he attempted to stimulate her. Sore and tired, but knowing it would be useless to resist, she submitted. The time it took for him to achieve satisfaction seemed, to her, an eternity. As he fell asleep she looked at the clock beside the bed. It was three-thirty.

CHAPTER TEN

Monday morning held a hint of impending winter. A light rain blanketed the rapidly discoloring leaves as they began their process of decay. Aaron Tidwell called David Allen Lester at seven forty-five in the morning. The conversation was brief and cordial. Could Mister Lester come in at one that afternoon? There were a couple of questions that had surfaced during the Cromwell investigation which needed his help to clarify. Lester stated he would be happy to assist. Tidwell thanked him and hung up the phone.

While Tidwell was speaking on the phone, Springs, wearing dirty clothes and driving a rusty dented truck, stationed himself in a surveillance location near the Lester's home. His job that morning was to follow the suspect and send an alarm if he attempted to leave the county. For his role he had foregone shaving over the weekend and his face was covered with two day stubble. The faded ball cap which hid the shortness of his hair completed his disguise.

Sawyer, contrary to his statement about getting rest, spent the weekend depleting his resources of owed favors in an attempt to acquire a conditional warrant. Backing off from his aggressive tactics to avoid the permanent burning of the bridges of friendship and cooperation, he reduced himself to reviewing what information they had and prepared to interrogate Lester. Agonizingly slow, the minutes until they would be face to face ticked by.

Precisely at one, David Allen Lester parked his vehicle in the courthouse lot and went inside. Chet Springs parked a block away and waited until Lester entered the building before locking the truck and making his way to his office. Ushered into the gray room, Lester took a seat, folded his hands in his lap and waited. Ten minutes later Sawyer and Tidwell opened the door and walked in.

"Mr. Lester," Sawyer began. "My name is Special Agent Sawyer and I am with the SBI. My office is in Asheville but I am temporarily assigned here in Jackson County. This is Detective Tidwell of the Jackson County Sheriff's office."

Lester rose and shook both their hands. He was dressed in a black denim long sleeve jacket that was buttoned to his neck. Worn kaki pants showed signs of paint stains. His tan work boots were scuffed and aged. The detectives made note of his shaven head, the lack of facial hair and the absence of hair on his hand. Ruggedly attractive, in his own way, the detectives instantly noticed the profundity of his eyes. They motioned for him to be seated.

"This should not take very long," Sawyer said as he took a seat. "Detective Tidwell and I, along with others, are investigating the Cromwell murders which occurred in January. Are you familiar with those murders?"

"I have read the papers and seen the news reports." Lester's voice was calm, confident, and relaxed.

"Good. Then I am sure you are also aware that these murders are part of a serial killer investigation which covers three states," Sawyer continued.

"Yes, I believe that I read that in one of the papers. Colorado and Arkansas I believe are the other two states."

"That's right," Sawyer said.

"Mr. Lester, are you cold?" Tidwell asked. "I think it's pretty warm in here and you are sitting there with your jacket buttoned. That makes me even warmer."

"I'm fine Detective. I suffer from poor circulation which tends to make my body cooler than average. I compensate by wearing warmer garments."

Tidwell thought the explanation questionable. "Okay. But if you get warm please feel free to take off your jacket."

"Thank you Detective, I will" Lester's eyes twinkled as he spoke.

"Now," Sawyer cleared his throat. "As I was saying; your name popped up during the investigation and we wanted to clarify the record. Have you ever lived in Colorado?"

"Yes I have," Lester answered with a smile.

"What about Arkansas?" Sawyer probed. "Have you ever lived there?"

"Yes." Lester nodded his head as he spoke.

"How long did you live in Arkansas?" Tidwell asked, watching for any type of reaction to his question. There was none.

"Maybe eighteen months, maybe two years."

"And before Arkansas, where did you live?" Sawyer asked.

"Colorado."

"You lived in Colorado before living in Arkansas?"

"Yes that's correct."

"When did you leave Arkansas?" In his mind Tidwell was computing the time frame.

"Oh, let's see now." Lester stroked his chin while thinking. "About four years ago I believe."

"And you moved to North Carolina from Arkansas?" Tidwell's face was one of skepticism.

Lester emitted a brief laugh. "No sir," he said. "My wife is from Colorado. She was homesick so we went back to Colorado and stayed there until her parents died."

"I'm sorry for her loss," Sawyer said. "How did they die?"

"Tragic accident, I'm afraid." Lester pursed his lips. "Their car plummeted off the side of a mountain killing them both instantly. Naturally the event absolutely devastated my wife. It was a tragic, tragic time for everyone."

"So you moved to North Carolina from Colorado about what, two years ago?" Sawyer asked.

"Not quite two years." Lester's facial expression revealed only a willingness to cooperate.

"Now Mr. Lester, what do you think about the fact that you lived in Arkansas when those murders were committed, you lived in Colorado when those murders were committed, and that you're here in North Carolina when these murders were committed? How do you explain that?" After asking the question Sawyer loosened his tie and leaned back in his chair.

"Happenstance, despite the obvious appearances it remains nothing more."

"That's an interesting choice of words," Tidwell injected. "Not many people use happenstance in their conversations. You must be an educated man Mr. Lester. Where did you go to college?"

The question brought another laugh from Lester. "Detective, one does not have to attend a university to have knowledge. The world is a classroom. The individual is responsible for learning from it. I pride myself on my self-education."

"I'm just a country boy myself," Tidwell remarked. "I'm not use to such big words so I'll put it like this. What you are telling us is that it was just dumb luck that you lived in the same states at the same time that nine people were murdered."

"Inopportune, but yes, that is what I am telling you. Dumb luck, as you say," Lester said in a patronizing way. "But I am equally certain that I am not the sole human to have lived in those states at the exact time of the unfortunate demise of those poor people."

"And you expect us to believe your presence in all three states was nothing but chance?" Sawyer asked.

"I'm sure if you had evidence to the contrary I would by now be incarcerated." For a fleeting second Tidwell thought he detected emotion in Lester's eyes. The moment passed as quickly as it emerged and the eyes reverted to their charming dance of entertainment.

"Mr. Lester will you give us your permission to search your house?" Tidwell's voice was low and soft but the question echoed like a gunshot off the walls surprising Sawyer.

Lester thought before responding. "If I decline then you automatically assume my guilt. If I consent you have an open invitation to confiscate my personal belongings with no legal standing except my gesture of cooperation. It is a no win situation. Rather than have you invade my privacy I will decline the offer and leave you with whatever assumptions your minds wish to formulate."

"Do you want to talk this over with an attorney?" Sawyer asked.

"Not necessary." Evident to both detectives was the fact that David Lester remained in control of his emotions.

"Before moving to Colorado the first time, "Tidwell asked, "where did you live?"

"Is it important?" Lester asked.

"Just trying to clear everything up," Tidwell replied. "I mean, hey, you told us it was just bad luck that you lived where people were being butchered and you want us to take you at your word, so how about helping us a little here? Taking people at their word, you know, that goes against our nature. So, where did you live before you lived in Colorado the first time?"

"California."

"And before that, where did you live?" Tidwell pressed.

"Nevada."

"Move around a lot do you?" Sawyer wanted to know. "You hiding from something or you merely want to see the country?"

"A bit of a nomad at heart I guess," Lester chuckled. "Although, America is blessed with beautiful scenery."

"That is a fact?" Tidwell attempted to catalog the man setting across from him. He had interrogated hundreds of suspects. Most could be placed in one group or another. Those who sweated. Those that were too obliging. Those who denied knowledge while squirming in their seats. Those that falsely confessed even though everyone knew they were innocent. Then there were those who were void of emotion. Effortlessly they deflected all questions and all theories while sitting nonchalantly watching their questioners go down in flames. Lester, he decided, fell into that grouping.

"How long did you live in Nevada?" Sawyer asked.

"Oh, I really do not recall." Lester cocked his head to the side. "I was young then. I think it was only briefly; hardly worth mentioning."

"And California," Sawyer quizzed, "What line of work did you do there?" He leaned back in his chair.

"I was a woodworker. A handyman I think you would call it. I was fortunate enough to find steady employment which paid a moderate compensation."

"I do like the way you talk, Mr. Lester," Tidwell said mockingly.

"No obscenities. I like that too. Most of the people I talk to can not string two words together without swearing."

"You must realize Detective," Lester replied. "The majority of the populace has an elementary mentality which requires them to interject short offensive words into their speech. The more offensive the word the more acceptable they perceive themselves to be. I am not burdened with that problem. My intelligence is much higher than theirs."

Sawyer was intrigued. "Have you had your IQ tested?" he wanted to know.

"Yes, of course."

"And what were the results? If you don't mind sharing with us that is." Tidwell leaned forward as he spoke, his eyes locked with those of Lester.

"One hundred and sixty-two."

The session lasted for five hours in which Lester repeatedly declined the need for legal representation. Coolly he denied his involvement in the murders, and repeatedly offered his cooperation. When it ended he stood and stretched. After shaking their hands he preceded to dispassionately walk to his car. Starting the engine he drove away from the courthouse.

Sawyer and Tidwell had gained only a little more information about their number one person of interest. Still, it was information which, if pursued, might reveal more information and possibly the key to the puzzle.

Watching Lester walk away both detectives felt confident that they had the right man. The calm gracious confidence he exhibited and the ease with which he deflected questions deepened their conviction. Both were struck by the coldness of his eyes. Dark blue knife-like spheres dissecting anyone or anything gazed upon. Both men had experience with the mentally deranged. Neither had experienced anyone like David Allen Lester. Other than the fact he was arrogant in his supremacy he fit no profile, no stereotyping. As vigilantly as governments have attempted to categorize humans throughout the years into certain groups and types, Lester stood in a class of one. Whatever his background, whatever his experiences, in the final summation both Tidwell and Sawyer concurred in their conclusions. Both were convinced that for the first time in their careers they had sat in the presence of pure evil.

"Will he run?" Tidwell asked.

Sawyer shook his head. "No, I don't think so. I think he is too confident. But I almost wish he would."

CHAPTER ELEVEN

The erroneously acceptable rational is that serial killers, unable to conform with society are unable to control their urges. Wanting to be stopped, their crimes are their bizarre cries for attention and help. Historically they have demonstrated the careless penchant of escalating actions to a degree of carelessness. Profilers and law enforcement personnel, along with certain members of the medical community, believe their demented and disturbed urges can not be healed by medical solutions. Only by imprisonment or execution can the mental attitudes be contained. Psychotherapy aided by prescription medication, they believe, only temporarily masks the desires. A convicted rapist forced to undergo medical castration which causes impotency continues to experience fantasies. The ability to perform is altered but the desire lives forever. But profiling is not without its failures or controversies. Sawyer, for all his achievements in the field, reluctantly admitted if Lester were indeed the perpetrator, his profile was far from accurate.

Finagling funds for investigative trips they left the surveillance of Lester in the hands of deputies. Sawyer boarded a plane to California, intent on gathering more information about their prime suspect. He believed the answers lay on the Pacific coast. Tidwell's ticket was to

Colorado. His mission was to gain information on the deaths of the victims and anything which could prove their paths crossed that of Lester's. Springs, taking Nevada, was to uncover Lester's trail while he resided in that state. Together they hoped to construct a time line that would be irrefutable; a time line which would detail a killer's path to his victims. "A needle in a haystack," was the words that stuck in their minds. Assisted by local authorities during the days, the team communicated nightly via conference calls from their motel rooms.

"Clair Johnston," Springs said into the phone after being in Pahrump, Nevada for a week.

"Who is she?" Sawyer asked.

"She worked in a local brothel. Evidently she befriended someone fitting Lester's description years ago. Took him in, fed him, you know all that nurturing stuff."

"What does she have to say about him?" asked Tidwell, speaking from his motel room in Silverthorne, Colorado. He sounded tired.

"She disappeared from sight, along with the guy she took in," Springs replied. "The missing person was filed by one of her friends. Her car surfaced in LA a couple of months after she went missing. There wasn't much left when it was found. The locals really didn't pursue it. Adults come and go all the time in her profession. Most people don't even notice. Same attitude as anywhere else I guess. Not a lot of resources for checking out missing hookers."

"Is there anybody else around who remembers her guy?" Sawyer wanted to know.

"Just a couple of older gals. They remember him as being gracious but weird. According to them he had two hobbies. Lifting weights and engaging in group sex. Neither of which are illegal in Nevada -between consenting adults I mean. When those activities bored him he would go with Clair to work, hide behind a curtain and watch."

"I wish I had something to report," Tidwell said. "Colorado authorities are helpful but as they keep reminding me they have turned over all their files."

"What about the wife's parents?" Sawyer quizzed hopefully. "Is there anything helpful in the accident reports?"

"Joe, I got to tell you, there's not a whole lot to tell. Their car took a nosedive off a mountain road and plunged about two thousand feet straight down. Burst into flames on impact. They did manage to recover the bodies, but the car is still there."

Sawyer persisted. "Are there any neighbors or co-workers willing to talk? They always know were the skeletons are."

"It's like prying open an oyster shell with just your fingertips," Tidwell retorted. "Same nonsense we got in Jackson County. Nice guy. Gracious. Cordial. Nothing but run of the mill stuff that neighbors usually say about murderers. Truth is I don't think they really knew him. They say he kept to himself for the most part. Or they just don't trust authority. Seems to be a lot of survivalists in this neck of the woods, you know. Anyway, in the morning I am going to the crime scene to get a first hand look. Maybe I can see something no one else has. What's happening in California?"

"I'm going to spend a few more days here kicking the curbs," Sawyer replied. "It is a good place to get lost. All the temptations any one person could ask for." He laughed. "Chet, why don't you head back to North Carolina? I don't think you are going to find out much more. Aaron can fly back after he sees the crime scene. I'll be back sometime this weekend. Once we all get home I think we should have another sit down with Lester."

"I think we should push him harder this time," Tidwell suggested. "Ask the same questions enough times he gets bored and then we'll throw in a zinger."

"As long as he doesn't lawyer up," Springs added.

"I do want to push him," Sawyer stated. "He may have ice in his veins but I want to see if we can trigger some reaction. We'll discuss it on Monday. See you in Sylva." He omitted saying the extra days were not entirely for investigative purposes. Plagued by fatigue and a sense of something being wrong he had scheduled a physical. Better to not publish the appointment he thought. There was no need to have anybody worry for no reason.

Reunited in their basement offices the task force members exchanged what information they learned during their trips. Besides the disappearance of Clair Johnston, Nevada was a dead end. Still it was another name they could use in their questioning. In Colorado, Tidwell found only one person to speak ill of Lester. His in-law's neighbor spat on the ground when asked about the type of person his neighbor's son-in-law was. "Don't trust him and won't trust him." With no specific reasoning Tidwell chalked it up to a conflict of personalities.

The house where the murders had taken place still sat empty. Taped off with yellow tape the two story structure stood silent and blank. Infested with cobwebs and dust from lack of use it was of little help. Tidwell described how he spent several hours going from room to room in an attempt to understand what occurred and how it had been possible. No sign of forced entry, no fingerprints, no usable fluids, no hairs, no fibers. The bed where they died, still stained with their deaths, mutely guarded the secrets.

On the outside the house resembled that of the Cromwell's. Situated in a clearing with no overhanging trees. Behind the house stood a steeply rising hillside that would be difficult to traverse. Tidwell doubted the assailant would have troubled to come down the slope. In front of the house lay the driveway, winding its way towards the road. On both sides, less than a hundred feet from the house were large stands of trees. Comprised mainly of second growth and scrubs the left side offered few places to wait with unlimited visibility. The only logical conclusion was that the killer concealed himself on the right side. Walking through the trees Tidwell emerged just as the ground slanted in a steep decline. Gaining access to the home site, he concluded, had required considerable effort.

Sawyer had, by his own admission, received an education in the LA night life. Riding with cops in unmarked cars he'd witnessed all things imaginable. His brother officers were eager to enlighten their out of town visitor with speech and action. But in the seediest parts of the city Sawyer acquired the most information. The name David Allen Lester was still known, although no one had seen him in years.

Briefly he was employed in the porn industry. Not as a cast member but as a set carpenter. He was fired for attempting to force himself on an actress. Still, he had made a lasting impact. Due to his well known perversions, and his willingness to destroy those who opposed him Lester was shunned by the more respectable members of the profession. Several people went missing; it was rumored, after standing up to Lester or denying him what he wanted. Like in Nevada, their social standing did not lend itself to prolonged investigations. In the end he maintained friendships with a mere handful of people. Sawyer had run a check of the names he had. None were residing in North Carolina.

A bouncer in an all nude club, who doubled as a confidential informant, mentioned that Lester became obsessed with a society known as Utopia. Pressed for more details the bouncer told them what he knew. Utopia was a secret society that buys girls from overseas and sells them to its members who use them for sexual pleasure. According to the informant Lester was a believer and, becoming a disciple he preached the benefits and freedoms the society offered. If real, the bouncer stated, then it was deep, deep underground. Who could know for sure? But if anyone could find them, Lester would be the one. He was that obsessed

"This is a dangerous man we have in our community," Sawyer stated summing up his report. "Failure to remove him is not an option. We have to find the evidence."

Having Lester consent to another interview was easier than they estimated. His charade of co-operating citizen still intact, he arrived at the courthouse on the Wednesday morning before Thanksgiving wearing a long sleeved turtleneck sweater. Again ushered into the gray room he sat quietly waiting for the detectives. An additional table had been installed in the room and sitting on it was a reel to reel tape recorder. A large microphone was placed in the center of the table where Lester sat waiting. When the detectives entered the room he stood to recognize them.

"Please, Mr. Lester, be seated," Sawyer said. Turning on the recorder he introduced the other detectives and informed Lester that, if he had no objections the session would be taped. Lester granted his permission.

"Mr. Lester," Tidwell said. "I want to inform you of your rights. You have the right to remain silent. Anything you say can and will be used against you in a court of law. You have the right to speak with an attorney, and to have an attorney present during any questioning. If you cannot afford a lawyer, one will be provided for you at government expense. Do you understand these rights as I have explained them?"

"I do," replied Lester, a smirk crossing his lips.

"Knowing and understanding your rights as I have explained them to you are you willing to sign a wavier?"

"Ernesto Miranda. He's the reason you have to do that you know." Lester's smirk turned into a smile as he spoke. "Yes I will answer your questions."

Tidwell took a seat while Sawyer and Springs left the room. They had predetermined that each officer would have an hour alone with Lester, subsequently rotating like tag team wrestlers in a match. "Do you know what happened to Miranda, Mr. Lester?"

"He was killed in 1976 in a barroom brawl I believe."

"And how do you know that?" Tidwell, despite his feelings toward Lester, was impressed with his knowledge.

"I read it somewhere. I thought it was very interesting. Don't you?

Tidwell ignored the question. "Would you be willing to take a polygraph examination?" he asked.

"Not admissible in a court of law," Lester countered. "I'm sure you're aware of that detective."

"How well did you know the Cromwell's?"

"I only know them by the knowledge I acquired from reading the papers."

"You never met them, never had any contact with them of any kind?" Tidwell's voice was composed.

"To my knowledge that is correct, and as I have established

detective, I have an above average intelligence. I would recall any contact between myself and the deceased."

"Ever been in their house?"

"No reason to have been. As I stated, I did not personally know them."

Tidwell changed topics. "Do you know Gordon Smith?"

"The name is familiar I must say." Lester tapped his fingers on the table. "Yes, the name is familiar."

"He is the neighbor of your dead in-laws. Do you know him?"

Lester nodded. "Yes, I do. Not a pleasant sort of fellow. Busybody is a word I think you would understand."

"How do you know Hans Griener?" Tidwell asked.

"A German? No I don't believe I do know Mr. Griener. Should I?"

"You've never exchanged letters or pictures or video tapes with him?"

Lester shrugged his shoulders. "No reason to. As I stated, I do not know him."

"You never received anything in the mail from him?" Tidwell rocked his chair backwards balancing it on two legs.

"Sorry, I must again say no. I do not know the gentleman."

"Ever receive anything in the mail from the Cromwell's?"

"No." Lester leaned his chair backwards mimicking Tidwell.

"Ever send the Cromwell's anything in the mail? Any pictures, video tapes, magazines?"

"No. Detective this really is becoming quite boring. Is there another topic which you wish to discuss?" He allowed his chair to move forward until it rested on all four legs. Tilting his head he said, "Detective, why don't you dispense with the inconsequential questions and ask me what you really want to know?"

Tidwell stared at Lester's face. A conceited leer stared back. Minutes ticked past as Tidwell endeavored to understand the emptiness that lived within Lester.

The door opened and Chet Springs walked in and seated himself by Tidwell. "Mr. Lester, I have another appointment right now. Detective Springs is going to ask you a few more questions. Is that okay?" Lester nodded. "Do you need anything? Water, Coffee, soft drink?" Lester responded with the shake of his head. "But before I go, I just want to ask you why you murdered the Cromwell's? Why did you have to do that? What did they do to you?"

Lester's head snapped backwards. His mouth opened wide and a high pitched chortle escaped his throat. "Bravo detective," he said after regaining his composure and looking at the two officers. "Bully for you. Finally you had the audacity to ask the single most important query of your career. But I fear my answer will bestow no glory to your name. I am truly sorry, detective, but I did not kill the Cromwell's."

"Mr. Lester," Springs spoke as he watched Lester's eyes dance with amusement. "Who is Clair Johnston?" Tidwell stood and left the room, closing the door behind him.

"Who?" asked Lester, as the dance in his eyes receded.

"Clair Johnston. Who is she?" Springs repeated.

For a split second Lester's eyes flashed from amusement to uncertainty. "Someone from my past," he quickly answered. "I had to find her name in my memory."

"So you do admit knowing her?"

"Yes, I know her." Lester smiled across the table at Springs. "She is a lovely lady."

"How well do you know her?"

"Intimately. We lived together for awhile. She taught me many things. I have nothing but respect for her."

"Did you kill her?" Springs asked.

"I had no knowledge that she is dead?" Lester sighed as if the thought of her death was too painful to bear.

"Was she a whore?"

"She is a working girl yes; one of many in the state of Nevada. It is an honest occupation there."

"Where is she now?" Springs' voice was a flat monotone.

"Oh Lord," Lester said shaking his head. "It's been years since I've seen her. I don't want to speculate as to her whereabouts. But if I were forced to, I would assume she continues to reside in Nevada."

"What would you say if I told you her body had been found?"

"That would sadden me." Again Lester sighed to emphasize his words.

"Describe your intimacy with her," Springs commanded.

"Please detective. You are neither my physician nor my confessor." The smirk returned to his face.

"Are you homosexual?"

"No."

"Have you ever had a homosexual encounter?"

"No detective. Please let me save you some time. Have I ever masturbated? Yes. According to acceptable science it is a normal act through puberty. Have I ever had intimate relations with another male? No. Next question please."

Sawyer entered the room and took a seat beside Springs. "Mr. Lester, would you like to take a break?" Lester shook his head no. "No. Okay. I need to speak with Detective Springs for a few moments. If you would excuse us?"

Together the detectives left the room shutting the door behind them. Sitting in silence Lester looked intently at the door. The faint whine of the recorders reels was the only sound. When the door reopened Sawyer rushed through. In his hand was a manila file. Settling into the chair directly across from Lester he opened the file. Taking several photographs from the file he spread them over the table so Lester could view them.

"Do you know what these are Mr. Lester?" Sawyer asked.

"I assume from their size and quality they are pictures of the crime scene," Lester said looking briefly at the photos.

"That's right, that's right," said Sawyer. "Now, I want you to take a real good look at them, okay? They're not very pretty are they?"

"Misfortune is rarely attractive Agent Sawyer."

Sawyer thought about Lester's choice of words. "Yes," he said, "A horrible unnecessary misfortune. Did you kill these people?"

"As I informed your colleague Detective Tidwell, absolutely not."

"Are you sure?" Sawyer continued. "Look at them. Look at the women. They are really attractive don't you think? A lot of men would say they were really hot. And look at the bodies. Come on man, not all women have bodies like that. Am I right?'

"Yes, they were attractive." Lester reluctantly agreed.

"Attractive!" Sawyer shook his head back and forth. "No, no! They were beautiful! It's okay to say that. It's nothing to be ashamed of. Christ, every man would want to crawl into bed with them. It's okay to feel that way. It's natural. You wouldn't turn down the chance to have your way with them would you? It's okay to say they were beautiful."

Lester's eyes shifted between the pictures and Sawyer's face. "Yes, agent, they were beautiful women."

With startling speed Sawyer banged his fist against the table. "Then why did you kill them!"

Lester sat quietly, Sawyer's outburst failing to rattle him. "I didn't," he stated.

"Tell me about the society." Sawyer ordered, his voice again relaxed and calm.

"What society?" Lester asked. "If you are referring to the society of mankind a considerable amount of time would be necessary. If you are referring to other societies then you must be more specific if you really desire an answer to your question." Lester's eyes twinkled from across the table. "But you really are not looking for answers are you detective?"

Sawyer returned the smile with one of his own. "Come now Mr. Lester, let's not be bashful. The society you became obsessed with in Los Angles. The secret society known as Utopia The society you would give your right testicle to belong to. That's right. I know about the society. You know where I found out? The same place you did, Los Angles. A lot of people there remember you and not to kindly I must say. Is that why you killed them? They belonged and you didn't?"

"As I stated before I did not kill anyone. Homicide is against the law as you are aware. I did not know them. And I do not know anything about this theoretical society."

"Do you know a bouncer by the name of Rubin?" Sawyer could detect no change in Lester's expressions. He yearned to have the ability to have his suspect hooked to a machine which would monitor his heart rate. Surely there had to be fluctuations.

"I really can not say if I do or if I do not. I have met so many people in my travels. Sadly I do not always remember their names. There are so many of them and only one of me."

Sawyer looked at the man sitting across from him. The entire day had been spent playing a chess match of cunning and intelligence. The exterior calmness Lester exhibited, Sawyer thought, could be nothing more than a façade. There could only be two explanations for it not to be a façade. The first would be that Lester continued to think himself in control. The second, which Sawyer hesitated to contemplate, would be that Lester was innocent. "Will you take a polygraph examination?" Sawyer finally asked.

"That question has been asked and answered," Lester informed Sawyer. "The answer remains as before – no."

"Can we have your permission to search your home?"

"Again, asked and answered. And again, the answer is no."

"Of your own free will, will you provide us a DNA sample?"

"No."

"Do you want an attorney?" Sawyer inquired.

"For the fifth time today, no." Lester sighed with contempt.

"Tell me about the porn industry. Is that where you were a handyman?"

"A perfectly legal trade," Lester boasted. "Yes. At times I worked on the sets of adult films."

"Mr. Lester, let's get something straight right now. Let's get it out in the open so everybody understands everybody. Can we do that?" Sawyer was exasperated.

"Of course," Lester cried out. "I have nothing to hide. That is what I have been attempting to communicate to you over the course of the last several hours."

"Good," Sawyer stated. "I want you to understand one thing, and one thing only. Myself, Tidwell, and Springs, we are professionals. We've been doing this a long time. We know what you did. You may think yourself smarter than us, and you are a smart bastard, there is no denying that; but at the end of the day don't misjudge us. Our intelligence is as great as yours. And we will prove, beyond a shadow of a doubt, that you are guilty." Turning off the recorder he held the door open for Lester. "Have a Happy Thanksgiving."

Afterwards the three detectives sat at their desks. During the marathon interrogation no one dented the invisible armor Lester appeared to have shielded himself in. Intelligent, well spoken, defiant, arrogant, patronizing. Once again Sawyer worked the phones attempting to obtain warrants for the Lester home. Once again he was rejected. No probable cause. No evidence linking Lester to the victims. No evidence putting Lester in the victim's home. No evidence. The words taunted their spirits. The lateness of the hour on a holiday eve did little to assist Sawyer's attempts. Frustrated, the detectives forced themselves to evacuate their offices. As they did they mumbled under their breaths, their incoherent grumbling directed towards idiot attorneys and judges.

CHAPTER TWELVE

Retreating habitually into his world of fantasy, he knew, was a temporary respite. Still he was restless. He increased their out of town trysts. She objected only when he abandoned her. Marooned in isolated dwellings she was compelled to pleasure the strangers. Reappearing after his all night absences he rewarded her and their hostess by demanding they submit to his desires. His absences were necessary to reconnoiter with privacy. In a rare rebellious moment she attempted to rebuke him. His cold stone looks quickly quelled any thought of revolt. She was trapped. Lacking the strength to exert any amount of self independence she had no alternatives. Her capitulation was predictable.

With Christmas only days away he stunned her by announcing he would be going out of town. Looking up from her dinner plate she asked if she would be going as well. Quietly he assured her the trip was for business and not pleasure. She returned to her meal and the silence. His restlessness persisted through the evening, his tensions not easing until he was in the car, driving north. The cold weather re-energized his spirits. Mentally rehearsing the impending events he paid little attention to the assortment of Christmas lights decorating the homes he passed. The sound of carols drifted from the radio.

The city of Wytheville, Virginia, was arranged at the intersection of Interstate 81 and Interstate 77. Lightly populated, fewer than eight thousand residents, the small town in the Great Appalachian Valley, was big in history. Named after George Wythe, a signer of the Declaration of Independence, the town, with its salt and lead mines, had been an indispensable assist to the Confederacy during the War Between the States. Elevated more than two thousand feet above sea level, the terrain of Wytheville and its surrounding communities remain ideal for isolated home sites where inquisitive neighbors are prevented from becoming too inquisitive.

Hiding his car in a neglected field barn, he retrieved his knapsack from the trunk and smoked a cigarette, allowing his eyes time to adjust to the darkness of the night. With the temperature dropping and the wind increasing he walked the half mile to the house. The moon was tucked under the clouds and he stood in the front yard searching for any signs of movement. Satisfied there was none he circled the house.

An aging two story wood frame structure, the house's antiquated locks were breached with little effort. Limited furnishings accommodated the ease of his travel throughout the ground floor. Halfway up the stairs he detected muffled sounds. Instantly he froze, ears straining to identify the origin. Muffled, hard to distinguish, the sound baffled him. Minutes crept by. Could it be, he thought. Realization and identification brought a smile to his lips. Humans, for whatever reasons, are creatures of habit. Habits make humans predictable. Predictability makes humans susceptible to anyone with the desire to stalk them. They were exactly where he thought they would be. They were engaged in the activity he thought they would be engaged in. Victims, he knew, are often volunteers. Cat like he continued upwards to the landing.

Moving down the hall, away from the sounds, he checked the other bedrooms for occupants, found none, then retraced his steps. In front of the open master bedroom door he lingered, enjoying the sounds. From behind his back he retrieved the pistol with his left hand. Inching his right hand across the door frame and along the interior wall he located the light switch. Taking a deep breath he crossed the threshold and flipped the switch in a single motion.

On the bed, naked and intermingled, the faces of the three, suddenly illuminated, dissolved into panic. Pulling four lengths of rope from his back pocket he tossed them to the older of the females. His instructions, enforced by the cocking of the gun, were given in a quiet but commanding voice. Satisfied that the male had been bound to his specifications he moved to the bed, ordered the youngest female to her feet and placed the gun barrel to her temple. "We are not going to have any problems here are we?" he asked. Through head shakes his captives indicated he would not. Acknowledging their response he stepped backwards, dropped his knapsack on the floor and said, "Okay, then."

The hours passed as planned until it happened. Forced to accommodate him by performing fellatio the girl lured him into believing she was a willing participant. Suddenly she bit down on his penis. Uncontrollably he screamed. Grabbing her hair he yanked until, tolerating the pain no longer, she also screamed. Still clutching her hair he dragged her from the bed and tossed her into the bathroom. He was furious. She had tricked him and she would pay for her actions. As the girl lay on the floor sobbing he pointed the gun at the older female, commanding her to join them. When she complied he closed the bathroom door. Both screamed when they heard the gunshot from the other room.

Driving away from the field barn he was in a callous mood. Circumventing Wytheville he restricted traveling south to back country roads. As he neared the state line a large explosion shook the car and he struggled to maintain control. The blowout had interrupted his mind games and forced him back to reality. Cursing, he pulled as far off the road as he could and stopped the car. Changing a flat was not in his scenario. It would delay him, throw off his time schedule and force him to hurry.

As he was removing the blown tire headlights appeared behind him. Looking up he saw the blue lights of the patrol car flash on. Stopping behind him the local police officer got out of his car. "Bad place to be changing a tire," the officer said shinning his flashlight on the rear of the car. "Need any assistance?"

"Thank you sir, but no," he replied nonchalantly.

"On a morning dark as this, it wouldn't take much for someone not to see you and run over you. I'll just stay until you are through."

"Thank you officer, I appreciate that," he replied.

"Well, it's pretty quiet around these parts. At least this gives me something to do.

"That's good," he said.

"What's good?" the officer asked.

"Being quiet around here, I mean." He smiled up at the officer as he worked the jack.

The officer laughed and shook his head. "Yes it is. Tell me friend, what has you out at this hour anyway?"

"I had to attend a funeral up in Winchester this afternoon," he lied. "I was just trying to get home in time for Sunday morning church."

"Oh. I'm sorry for your loss. I'll just stay here and make sure your okay."

Finished, he tossed the split tire into the trunk, slammed it closed and again thanked the officer for his assistance. Alone and again moving southward he sucked vigorously on his cigarette saying a silent prayer of thanks that the country cop had not seen the butt of the pistol protruding from his pocket. He said a small thank you for not having to use it.

Pulling into his yard before sunrise he yawned. He arrived in time to keep his promise and escort her to church. Everything, he said to himself as he exited the car, goes well with a plan. And when it doesn't you improvise. Always have a contingency. Circumstances demanded it. Stretching and twisting from the prolonged sitting of the trip he entered the house, disrobed by the washing machine and threw his clothes in. After taking a shower he settled into bed next to her. Instinctively she moved, repositioning her body closer to his. Under the covers he snuggled close to her drinking in her smell.

CHAPTER THIRTEEN

News of the Wytheville murders was anything but welcomed by the three detectives in Jackson County. Uninvited, the Federal Bureau of Investigation was quickly on the scene. Once there, they assumed command with their natural talent for attracting media attention. The fact they had not been asked was, to them, irrelevant. Those who objected were ignored. Applying pressure on city and county officials, those whose theories differentiated from theirs were quietly assigned to other duties. The media frenzy and hyped panic that transformed Sylva now transformed Wytheville. The distinction between the two communities was uncomplicated - the FBI welcomed the excitement. J. Edgar Hoover, a rampant manipulator of the press would have been proud.

Almost as quickly as they swarmed the streets of the shocked town, the FBI issued a profile of their unknown suspect. "A single white male between the ages of thirty and forty; will be above average in height and strength. The suspect will be a smoker, probably a heavy drinker, and will have received limited education. Unable to hold a steady job, the suspect will probably be a loner lacking the social skills necessary to form relationships. He will have been abused as a child. Without question the abuse affected his normal thought patterns causing the antisocial behavior. He will be poor. He will have low self esteem. He murders to achieve feelings of power and manhood. The sexual elements of the crimes are secondary in nature, not the primary reason for the killings. They are added due to his inability to have normal sexual relations because of impotency."

Reading the profile Sawyer had a growing feeling of sickness in his stomach. Respectful of the Bureau's profilers he thought them to quick to placate communities and arrange themselves in positions to appear flawless. But their shortcomings and failures were many. The bombing during the Atlanta Olympics stood as an example of their failures. An innocent man's life was destroyed due to their erroneous profile. But to the loyal agents the Bureau and only the Bureau mattered.

To Sawyer what mattered most was how Lester evaded surveillance. Log books of assigned officers were checked. Dates, times, signatures; everything appeared to be in order. Lester had, once at home, not left until the next morning. His destination was church services with his wife. Alibis of that strength were hard to argue against in a courtroom. In desperation the officer on duty was summoned for questioning. In the end the consensus was that Lester was home. In the end the forced consensus was that Lester was not their man. At the insistence of the Sheriff the surveillance detail was ended.

A few days after the latest murders Sawyer and Springs were recalled to their duties with the SBI. During their last group conversation they discussed the fact that something had triggered a change in the time pattern of the killer. Cut in half, the new time sequence proved an indication of the killer's confidence in eluding detection. It could also, they agreed, be an indication that he was slipping deeper into his perverseness. It was not uncommon for organized killers to display unorganized traits as their unattainable needs took control over rational thoughts. The reduction of time between murders was a clear signal that others would follow in ever decreasing cooling off periods.

Aaron Tidwell remained a task force of one but was obligated to oversee other investigations as well. Wytheville's sorrow bolstered the predominate feeling in Jackson County that the killer had moved on. As Christmas approached, residents felt their lives return to the ordinary. Individual freedoms which accompany normalized activities were welcomed back in the minds of the citizenry. Aaron Tidwell stood out as the lone voice of disagreement. Forced to concede that Lester was not responsible he unyieldingly believed the executioner remained in their area. His rational was simplistic. If Lester was not the man now wanted in four states the true suspect had no reason to be uprooted. Clearly no one held a clue to his identity. That meant he remained safe from arrest. That also meant he was probably laughing at their utter confusion. The thought angered Tidwell.

Two weeks after entering the case, acting on a hot line tip, the FBI apprehended Jonas Milligan, a thirty-four year old single white male living in Lexington, Virginia. A heavy smoker and frequent patron in local barrooms, Milligan was barely literate having dropped out of middle school and running away from an abusive home life. A drifter by nature, Milligan was prone to mistrust his fellow man. Because of recurring episodes of hostility his one adult relationship ended when his live-in girl friend obtained an order of protection against him. In his possession, at the time he was taken in for questioning, was a twenty-two caliber revolver and a generic spool of rope which was comparable to that used in the crime. Resisting arrest cemented the agents belief he was guilty. Pointing to him as proof of their expertise in profiling, Milligan's shackled walk into jail was nationally televised.

Congratulating themselves for the speedy conclusion the FBI recalled their field agents and withdrew from the case. The Jackson County Sheriff made a point of mocking Tidwell in front of others. "See Tidwell," he said. "Two weeks and the FBI have a suspect in custody. In two weeks they did what you and the others couldn't do in a year."

A month later Milligan's court appointed attorney had all charges dismissed. Ballistics proved the gun was not the one used in the murder. Testimony from informants was suspect. Under examination, the statements proved fraudulent. With no other evidence the judge was left with little choice but to release the accused.

Milligan was euphoric in his release. He was also ostracized by his friends. Worse was being ignored by the same media who prior to his release had been fighting one another for an exclusive interview. Jonas Milligan was jobless, friendless, and penniless. Declining his attorney's suggestion to file a wrongful imprisonment suit, Milligan sought refuge in alcohol. A week after his release he walked in front of a speeding semi. His tribulations had ended.

Wythe County and the Wytheville police department breathed a sigh of relief when Milligan refrained from filing the lawsuit. That relief was short lived as they realized they were left to continue the investigation on their own. Aaron Tidwell understood their sudden feelings of inadequacies. For a year he had shared in those same feelings. Vainly he argued for the reinstatement of the task force. Vainly he argued for one other officer to be assigned with him. In vain, in vain, in vain. Every approach he attempted was in vain.

Discouraged and annoyed by the games of bureaucratic systems, he packed the files into boxes.

In doing so he questioned himself. Who was the killer? Where would he strike next? When would he strike next? He could not answer a single question. More often than comprehended by the public, luck plays a role in solving crimes. Good detective work and good luck. At times the good work just isn't enough. He wondered if he would have any of the luck. They zeroed in on one suspect, a suspect they had followed every minute of every day for months. But in the end, in the final analyzes, their one suspect was cleared by the officers assigned to watch over him. Only God and the Devil could be in two places at once. Tidwell knew Lester was not God. Neither, it was reluctantly apparent, was he the Devil. Tidwell sighed. Lady luck proved to be a jokester. After having the files transported to the hallways of his office he closed the doors on the basement of the courthouse for the last time.

CHAPTER FOURTEEN

Denver is a modern day major metropolis. But along with its size and population density comes the task of enforcing the law. To facilitate that enforcement the city is divided into six police districts, the airport segregated into its own separate district. District three, whose boundaries are East Colfax Avenue to the north, Belleview Avenue to the south, South Downing Street to the west, and West Dayton to the east, witnessed a sixty-six percent rise in homicides and a ten percent increase in sexual assault from 2006 to 2007. Not a district for the timid or squeamish, the third required dedicated and skilled officers.

Following a vehicle with an inoperative tail light, rookie officer Sean O'Malley flipped on the blue lights of the patrol car. Beside him, Albert Dennison, a veteran of ten years, ran a check of the license plate. Learning the vehicle was reported stolen the month before, Dennison engaged the siren. O'Malley accelerated to keep pace with the stolen vehicle. Weaving down one street, then up another, Dennison radioed for additional units.

Speeding down East Arkansas the fleeing vehicle made a sharp turn on a side street and emerged on East Iowa. Passing East Mexico and East Florida, the driver slammed on the brakes, spun the vehicle into a right hand turn that sent it up on two wheels before settling back on all four tires heading west on East Louisiana. Failing to negotiate another turn at high speed the driver slammed the vehicle into a parked car, the impact spinning him into a three sixty. Adrenalin coursed through his body. When the car stopped he opened the driver's door and, holding a nine millimeter in his right hand, emerged from the disabled car.

O'Malley braked the cruiser to a full stop twenty yards from the stolen vehicle. Dennison exited through the right door, O'Malley through the left, pulling his service weapon as he crouched behind the open door. Dennison, armed with a twelve gauge shotgun ordered the suspect to drop the weapon. As seconds ticked by with no response, the order was repeated. In the distance the cry of additional sirens signaled backup was nearby. The lights of another cruiser distracted Dennison momentarily. Seeing his opportunity, the suspect turned and ran.

O'Malley, the youngest of the officers on scene, had been a track star during high school and excelled in physical training at the academy. Instinctively he bolted from behind the car door in pursuit. Quickly he distanced himself from Dennison, who, still holding the shotgun, followed behind. At the corner the suspect halted, turned, leveled his gun at O'Malley then fired four rounds. The first two slammed into O'Malley's vest, their impact spinning him to the left and backwards. Raising his right arm he was able to return fire before the third shot from the suspect entered his underarm, bounced downward, splintered a rib, and came to rest in his lung. Reflex and training enabled him to return fire for a second time before the fourth and final round from the suspect penetrated his skull. Dead before his body could collapse onto the sidewalk, he never knew that his return fire found its mark. His last shot before dying crippled the suspect. Dennison found both in pools of their own blood.

Given medical treatment at the scene and transported to the hospital for surgery, the suspect was placed under armed guard with instructions for no admittance of visitors. A search of the vehicle uncovered an array of automatic weapons, drug paraphernalia, and pornographic materials to include videos of child pornography. Sixty-five thousand dollars in cash was also recovered.

Alberto Gonzales recovered from his wounds sufficiently to be transferred to the detention center where he was held without bail as he awaited trail. Aware he would face the death penalty he informed his court appointed public defender that he held information on a serial killer that authorities in four states would be interested in. But the death penalty had to be taken off the table or he would go to his grave with what he knew. His attorney, a seasoned litigator, although nauseated by Gonzales, had no option but to talk to the district attorney.

The DA was escorted into the room by two burly prison guards. In the room Alberto Gonzales, dressed in the orange jumpsuit inmates are forced to wear, and his attorney waited. Standing across from them the DA spoke. "It's your meeting. What do you want?" Clearly angry, the DA's voice was curt.

"My client has information," the public defender stated, "on murders in three different states."

"Is that right?" The DA's face showed his skepticism. "What kind of information?"

"The identity of the serial killer," replied the defense attorney.

"Really!" The DA shouted as he locked eyes with Gonzales. "And what serial killer would that be, Mr. Gonzales?"

Gonzales' voice was raspy. "Arkansas, North Carolina, and Virginia. Check it out; you'll see I'm right."

"I'm aware of those investigations," the DA responded as he positioned himself in a chair. "But that does not change the fact that you murdered a police officer right here in this city. The mayor's demanding justice."

"The mayor's demanding vengeance," Gonzales' attorney responded, his voice matching the anger of the DA's. "And you know that's not the same thing."

"You're splitting hairs are you counselor? Justice or vengeance, in this case it really doesn't matter. What do you want?" The DA looked back at the attorney.

"Take the death penalty off the table. Mr. Gonzales will plead guilty to the shooting of Officer O'Malley and agree to life without parole but you can't stick a needle in his arm."

The DA snickered. "You've got nerve Gonzales. And what do I tell the Mayor and the Police Commissioner, and the thousand cops looking for your blood?"

"Tell them this is for the greater good," Gonzales said.

"I have to take it to my boss," the DA said, attempting to delay what he knew would be inevitable.

"Take it to the damn Governor, if you want," Gonzales spouted. "But I don't say shit until we have a deal."

The DA sighed then leaned back in his chair. "This better be good Mr. Gonzales or all bets are off. Okay, let's here it. What's his name and how do you know him? And let me tell you this better not be bullshit! Understood?"

Gonzales looked at his attorney and waited until he nodded approval before he spoke. "His name is Caleb Rousseau."

CHAPTER FIFTEEN

Memorial Day Weekend in Jackson County is the traditional kick-off of the summer season. Saturday mornings in the cubicles of the Sheriff's office were habitually quiet times. Aaron Tidwell sat at his desk poring over the files of the Cromwell murders, a sacrament he preformed countless times. That afternoon he had scheduled a get away with his wife and he was looking forward to the long over due reprieve from business. Surprised to see the Sheriff standing in front him he came to his feet.

"I just got off the phone with the Denver Chief of Police," the Sheriff stated. "They're holding a cop killer named Alberto Gonzales. Ever hear of him?" Tidwell shook his head no. "No? Well, he's heard of you. He also has evidence in the Cromwell case. Ever hear of Caleb Rousseau?" Again Tidwell shook his head. "According to Gonzales, Rousseau is the man you've been looking for."

Tidwell was skeptical. "And how does he know that?"

"He's got a damn video tape of the murders. He claims Rousseau sent it to him." The Sheriff muffled a yawn. "There's a flight from Asheville to Denver at six tonight. I've got you booked on it. Go have a sit down with Gonzales and bring back that tape." He started to leave then stopped. "This is an election year Tidwell. I don't have to tell you what that means. Understand?" Tidwell nodded. He'd heard the veiled threats before. "Good." With that the Sheriff was gone.

Seated in the rear of the plane, Tidwell felt mixed emotions. Elated that a possible break in the case could be forthcoming he was conflicted by the stress his departure, together with the uncontrollable quantity of time the case demanded, had had on his family life. The cancellation of the planned weekend retreat was not received well. The atmosphere at home was strained to the breaking point. Good-byes were cool, quiet and subdued.

Professionals in all occupations have stress. Professionals in all occupations, from time to time, carry that stress home. It is only natural that, once inside the home, it affects relationships. Career related stress in a policeman's life is compounded dramatically when involved in a high profile case. Fending off the daily bombardment from all sides, public, political, and professional, requires Herculean resolve and dedication. The involuntary consequences of those efforts often affect loved ones.

Shaking off the feeling of self-pity, Tidwell evaluated what he learned in the hours before taking his seat on the aircraft. Gonzales had used the tape as his ace in the hole. Knowing the value of the tape and knowing that the authorities would be willing to forfeit deserved justice for possession of the evidence, he had secreted it in an airport locker. Only after a written and signed agreement was in place did he give up the locker number and the name of the individual holding the key. When the airport district officers opened the locker they recovered the tape. Still in the manila envelope it was mailed in, it was the only thing in the locker. The reddish blue post mark, dated three months after the murders, was from Georgia. The only prints they found belonged to Gonzales.

Agreement signed, tape recovered, Gonzales did an about face and refused to cooperate. He would answer no more questions. Threatened with having the plea bargain revoked he reluctantly consented, to speak with one officer of his approval. From seemingly nowhere he named Aaron Tidwell as the only cop he would talk to. Political and judicial jousting lasted several days before the Colorado authorities conceded the tape contained nothing of consequence to aide their own investigation and made the call to North Carolina. Aware of scarcely buried feelings of duplicity felt by the Denver police force towards the district attorney, Tidwell was cynical about the reception and cooperation he would receive.

The last passenger to disembark, Tidwell was met by a tall man dressed in civilian clothes who introduced himself as a special investigator with the DA's office. The greeting was cordial but, as expected, reserved. With no checked luggage to retrieve the duo quickly made their way through the airport. Outside they were met by an unmarked car whose driver wore the uniform of Denver PD. Within a half an hour, a ride that was remarkable only by its punctuated silence, Tidwell was dropped at his motel with instructions to be ready at eight the next morning.

Settled into his room Tidwell picked up the phone and made two calls. The first was to Joe Sawyer. Sawyer had been diagnosed with pancreatic cancer. Resigning from the day to day routine of the SBI he now worked occasionally as an agency consultant. Respecting his insights and opinions, Tidwell routinely provided his friend updates on the case which had thrown them together. The conversation lasted for forty-five minutes. The second call was to his wife to let her know that he arrived safely and hoped to be home in a couple of days.

According to phone records the duration of their call was one minute and twenty-nine seconds.

Punctually at eight the same dark unmarked sedan pulled up at the motel. Tidwell, unable to sleep, had been up for hours. He was waiting with an unlit cigar in his mouth. The same driver and same escort again declined unnecessary conversation. As the car wove through the streets of the city Tidwell stared out the window. Arriving at the jail the plainclothesman and Tidwell entered through the front, signed in, and checked their weapons. Buzzed through the first set of bars, Tidwell was immediately surrounded by four guards who escorted him through the corridors. Ushered into a barred and wired room that housed a table and four wood chairs, the guards left Tidwell to wait for Gonzales.

Placing his briefcase on the table the detective took a seat. Almost instantly the door was buzzed opened and Alberto Gonzales, dressed in the jail's orange jumpsuit and wearing ankle shackles and handcuffs, shuffled in. Correctional officers held his arms as they directed him to a specific chair, sat him down, and cuffed him to the table. Accompanying Gonzales was his attorney. When the guards were gone, Gonzales spoke. "So you're Detective Tidwell?"

A small man barley five-six in heeled shoes, Gonzales was dark skinned, with brown eyes, and a mop of unkempt black hair which hung to his shoulders. Tidwell coolly looked into his eyes and saw amusement instead of anticipation. On the streets in the midst of an unsuspecting populous, Tidwell knew, he could be a dangerous man.

"And you are Alberto Gonzales, the cop killer," Tidwell said, looking for a reaction.

"Alleged," the attorney interjected. "The final allocution has not yet taken place."

Gonzales smiled. "A rookie cop; what kind of fucking luck is that?"

"I really don't care," Tidwell replied. "That's not why I'm here. Every cop in this city wants to strap you to a gurney and stick a needle in your arm. I don't care. You understand?"

"That's cool." Gonzales said as he looked at his attorney and nodded.

"Detective Tidwell," the attorney began. "My client will answer all of your questions to the best of his ability. In return we need you to affirm to the local authorities that he has willingly cooperated in your investigation."

"Until I hear what he has to say I don't guarantee anything," Tidwell replied. "I've come a long way just to be jerked around."

The attorney nodded his understanding.

Taking a legal pad and a tape recorder from his briefcase Tidwell placed them on the table. Pushing record he said, "Tell me about Caleb Rousseau."

"He is a crazy mother, that one," Gonzales laughed. "No fear, no remorse, no feelings. He would be happier to kill you than talk with you."

"How do you know him?" Tidwell's eyes were glued to Gonzales.

"We met in LA. I was running with this whore who was stepping out on me. CR, that's what I call him, CR was the bastard she was stepping out with. He nearly beat me to death."

"Doesn't sound like you two were friends to me," Tidwell

interjected. "So you're getting back at him now with this fairy tale, is that it?"

"I got over my jealous streak and we started hanging out. We even tagged teamed a couple of whores occasionally." Gonzales smiled at the memories.

Tidwell wasn't amused. "Is that how you get new friends, having them kick the crap out you?" he asked.

"You don't understand, man," Gonzales' smile vanished. "He was really into that, you know, sex with a lot of different people at the same time. He worked in the porn business. That dude has amazing staying power. Chicks love it."

"When was the last time you saw him?" Tidwell wanted to know.

"Shit man, I don't know for sure. Been a few years now. It was right before he left LA. He went off in search of some society."

"How did he know where to send the tape, if it had been that long ago? You two stay in touch?"

"I got a P. O. box. I check it every couple of months. He knew the address. The tape just showed up." Gonzales turned his hands palm up. "Honest."

"How do you know the tape was from him?"

"Because of the letter he wrote," Gonzales sneered. "Hell, you're not to smart for a cop."

Tidwell ignored the remark. "You still have the letter?" he asked.

Gonzales laughed. "Hell no! Do I look like a fucking librarian? I tossed it after I read the thing."

"You watch the tape?" Tidwell wanted to know.

Gonzales shook his head. "I read the letter and put the tape in the locker. I thought it might buy my freedom some day. Shit! A rookie cop! No fucking freedom from that."

Tidwell stared at the stubble on Gonzales' face. "Then how do you know what's on the tape, if you didn't watch it?"

Annoyed at the question Gonzales blurted, "Because of the letter!"

Tidwell changed subjects. "Did he ever talk about his childhood? Where he grew up, where he was born, anything like that?"

"Once," Gonzales answered. "We were just hanging, smoking some weed and having some beers. But I didn't believe what he said."

"And why is that?"

"It was too bizarre. Dude, no kid is growing up fucking his aunts every night. Shit like that just don't happen." Gonzales shook his head.

"Did he say where his aunts lived?"

Nodding his head, Gonzales attempted to recall the conversation. Finally he said, "Oh yeah, someplace outside of New Orleans. Some hick town. Something west."

"Westwego?" Tidwell asked, his brow rising in recognition of the name.

"Westwego? Westward? Yeah, could be," Gonzales said. "I know it was west something. Been along time since that night. I don't know for sure. I do remember him yakking about mumbo jumbo voodoo bullshit he said his aunts were into. He said a lot of crazy things you know. He was in some kind of fantasy freak show out in LA with another dude. I was so juiced during those days, hell, I couldn't tell you red from blue. After awhile I don't think he could tell what was real and what wasn't

"Was he into drugs as well as sex?"

There was another laugh from Gonzales. "Oh, he did his share of drugs alright, but his thing was sex. Everything was about the sex. He thought every bitch should give it up whenever he wanted it. As I said we shared some ass a few times."

Tidwell thought for a moment. "Do you know when he left home? Left his aunts' home?"

"He said he was fifteen. Ran away, lived on the street. That kind of bullshit" Gonzales shrugged. "But you could never tell when he was lying."

"What about this society -Utopia? Does it exist?" After making notes on his legal pad Tidwell leaned back.

"I didn't think so at first you know? I mean, how cool would that be, if it was real you know. Getting all the pussy you wanted, swapping it around, getting the young stuff. Man that would be the righteous life. So that's why I didn't believe it. Shit like that don't happen in Hell." Gonzales' eyes went blank and his voice lowered to a whisper. "That's what this world is you know. Hell! Everybody is just walking through Hell. But it's real! CR found the bastards. He sent me some stuff on it. It's very real."

"Is he a member?" Tidwell wanted to know.

"That's the problem. All the members are smart educated people with their heads screwed on straight. Lack of education fucked him." Clearing his throat, Gonzales lifted his eyes towards the ceiling. "CR talks the talk but he can't cut the education bullshit. They check on all that shit you know. That's what pissed him off so much. The bastards wouldn't let him in. They slammed the door in his face man and, oh shit- that's a bad thing to do to CR. He wanted to kill all of them that night."

"What about the girls? Where do they get the girls?"

Gonzales smiled widely. "That's the beauty of it all. They buy them.

Their parents don't want them so they sell them to this company in Canada or their runaways that get scooped up by slave traders. World wide sex for sale, how great is that? Happens all the time you know. The company gets them, fixes them, so there's no rug rats' popping out, then educates them, that's what they call it, educating them; then they sell them to society people. Everybody's happy." Gonzales laughed. "What a fucking life!"

Tidwell fought to restrain his feelings of nausea. "How did Rousseau find out about them?"

"He has luck. Just plain stupid luck. He always was a lucky bastard." Suddenly Gonzales frowned. "If I had his luck I wouldn't be here." He shook his chains to emphasize his surroundings.

"And you don't know where he is right now?" Tidwell asked, knowing what answer he would get.

"Sorry."

"And you had nothing to do with the crime on the tape or any prior knowledge? Is that what you want me to believe?"

"Hell, I've never been to North Carolina. People talking funny and all that shit, playing banjoes, and marrying their sisters. Hell no, I didn't have anything to do with it."

"Can you describe Rousseau to a sketch artist?"

Gonzales looked at his attorney and waited for a gesture of approval before answering. "It's been along time, but…" he paused. "Yeah, I guess so."

Tidwell turned to the attorney. "How soon can you arrange for your client to sit down with a sketch artist?"

"Possibly this afternoon, I suppose," the attorney replied.

Tidwell turned back to Gonzales and said, "Alberto, if you've told me one lie, or have been jerking me around in any way, you know what's going to happen?" Gonzales nodded. "Okay, while your attorney is arranging for the artist let's start again"

The questioning consumed ten hours of the day. Gonzales's attorney excused himself long enough to arrange for an artist to be standing by. While Tidwell packed his briefcase, the artist, a young man who was visibly uncomfortable being inside a jail, hastily drew on his pad what Gonzales verbalized. Satisfied the rendering was an acceptable representation of Caleb Rousseau, Gonzales handed it to Tidwell. It was the eyes in the drawing that instantly affected the detective. The face looked strangely familiar. The eyes were unusual, mysterious, and deceptive. He questioned the accuracy of the black and white drawing. Gonzales assured him that was his man.

"One more question," Tidwell said preparing to leave "This company, as you call them, the one supplying the girls. Have they got a name?"

Gonzales grinned. "Everything has a name man. I just don't know what it is."

Tidwell took one last shot. "And you don't know where Rousseau is right now?"

"Not a clue."

Outside Tidwell was picked up at the jail's entrance, handed a brown envelope, seated in the back of the car and driven to the airport. After going through security there was under an hour to wait before boarding. Telephoning Joe Sawyer he relayed the description of the face in the sketch. He had never seen the face before. He had, it dawned on him, seen troubled eyes very similar. But those eyes belonged to a man circumstances proved innocent. Having already memorized the sketch he knew he would never forget the face. Boarding the plane he was optimistic. As the plane lifted from the tarmac he fell into a state of exhausted sleep.

CHAPTER SIXTEEN

The light of the moon cascaded through the stand of hemlocks and intermittently illuminated the ground beneath the trees. He was standing motionless, arms upraised. Oblivious to his surroundings he remained in his catatonic like state. In his mind the panoramic images of those he attempted to educate and liberate perpetually repeated themselves. Each image he held sacred, as he did each memory of the sounds and smells. As if happening at that moment, he could feel the sensations massage his flesh and feel the warmth of their breath upon his face. Knowing they would always be his companions comforted him and he cherished the thought.

Lowering his arms he moved quietly through the trees avoiding the low hanging branches. Arriving at his observation point and crossing his legs, he lowered himself to the ground where he began a rocking motion. In his line of vision he could see the house, the barn like out building, and the front yard. Interior lights tossed shadows on closely planted shrubbery. Sporadically someone would pass a window and he would focus on their size and shape. He counted them as they appeared - one, two, three different forms. Realization the forms represented three different people drifted within his brain.

Could they be the ones, he thought to himself. Could they be the true believers? Oh how he longed for his hopes to be true.

Suddenly a fourth person passed by the windows. The manifestation froze him from his rocking. His mind raced with unanswered questions. Conjecture and hypothesis twisted his thoughts in a multitude of directions. Unexpected and unexplained the fourth person presented exceptional opportunities and exceptional risks. The idea further aroused him. Forcing himself to calmness he stood and inched closer to the tree line. Closer - he must get closer. Slowly he inched his way towards the house. He could hear sounds from inside. It was the sounds of music, singing, and the boom of a base guitar. Like a magnet the sounds drew him closer.

Another figure appeared by the window. Fearing detection he dropped to the ground. Laying prone he stared at the house. The figure remained by the window gently swaying with the music. There were five people! His heart raced. Sweat dripped from his forehead into his eyes, the salty content temporarily blinding him. Never had he experienced such profuse sweating. The perspiration frightened him.

Using his hands he pushed himself backwards. Rocks and twigs littered his path. Their rough sharpness tore at him and penetrated his clothing. His skin was gouged. Warm blood oozed from his skin. Panic knocked at his soul. Afraid to rise he continued with his backward push towards the safety of the trees. A rock punctured the palm of one hand and then the other. Looking over his shoulder he could see the trees getting closer, their nearness begging him to push harder and faster.

Biting his lip to prevent crying out in pain he pushed himself to his feet. He turned ready to run. Instantly the area was flooded with light. Faceless people were everywhere. Armed with clubs and rocks they surrounded him. His own scream woke him from the nightmare.

Wheezing heavily, he lay in the sweat soaked sheets trying to slow the beat of his heart. Beside him he could feel the shift of her body. Rising he fumbled for a cigarette, lit it, then moved through the house to the back door. Outside, standing on the deck, the coolness of the night air evaporated the perspiration from his body. Taking deep breaths he drank in the coolness, allowing it to wash his mind.

This night reminded him of the night in Colorado. It was the same coolness, the same temperature. The same formation of clouds partially blocking the stars. The thoughts drew him back in time.

They were spontaneous people. To learn their movements, their routines, he was challenged. But determination overcomes challenge. In the end he succeeded. The draft of his plans required factoring in additional time. Scaling the steep incline with the backpack was exerting. Profusely perspiring he reached the trees winded, needing to catch his breath. The night's cool air helped cleanse his face and dry his clothing. Knowing his struggles would be rewarded he stood calmly waiting, watching the house.

Through the windows he could see them, their movements fueling his expectations. Beautiful, he kept repeating to himself. Beautiful. They had natural beauty without need of artificial enhancement; figures of statuesque perfection complimented by unblemished flesh. During his research he, at one point, ventured close enough to hear them talking. The softness and purity of their voices were angelic, their laughter comforting. He was fearful his hopes for them would be unfeasible. Only time would unmask the truth.

Emerging from the trees at the appropriate time he easily gained access to the house. Their startled expressions were replaced by those of fear. Those were then replaced by expressions of obedience.

Temporarily he experienced perfection. Temporarily he unearthed the Garden of Eden. Ultimately his residency in that garden was denied. The rejecters required punishment; punishment and freedom. Punishment for their bigotry and their absence of purity; freedom from their earthly limitations. Their destinies complete, he kissed them softly, inhaling the fragrance of their beings.

The memories left him weak yet with a sense of satisfaction. He finished smoking another cigarette then returned to the bedroom. Not wanting to awaken her he slid into bed quietly. Rotating to his side he laid awake deep in thought listening to her soft snoring. Near dawn she shifted again, snuggling against his back. They had been together for nine years and he had grown accustomed to her presence, to her agreeableness to participate in his desires. But lately he witnessed a recent change in her way of thinking and it gave him pause. He also noticed a change in her appearance, a slight increase in weight, a sag in her breasts, a widening of her buttocks. As he drifted back to sleep he made a mental note to confront her about her transgressions in the morning.

CHAPTER SEVENTEEN

Aaron Tidwell was uncomfortable sitting in the Asheville offices of the FBI. Listening to an orientation on human trafficking his mind repeatedly strayed to the whereabouts of Caleb Rousseau. Beside him sat Joe Sawyer.

Short and curvy with black hair and thick glasses, Eileen Donner, the agent assigned to handle the information Tidwell brought back from Denver appeared very conversant on the subject. Despite her young age she was, to Tidwell's appreciation, explaining in detail the multibillion dollar industry.

Her orientation began with the statement that trafficking in humans posed a multi-dimensional threat. Keeping the education to the basics she explained how it deprives people of their human rights and freedoms. How it increases the chance of global health issues. How it spawns the growth of organized crime. Unknown to the general public is the fact that annually about six hundred to eight hundred thousand people, mainly women and children, are trafficked across national borders. The majority of those sold end in the trade of sex. That was not to say, she reminded them, that adult males are never trafficked because they are. Usually for the men, the purpose is slave labor. The numbers did not include those who were trafficked within the boundaries of their own countries. That number remains unknown. Realistically the true number of trafficked humans exceeds a million every year.

Countries are rated, she explained, on a tier system; one through three. The rating, one, is given to countries demonstrating no tolerance for trafficking. Tier one countries have established laws against the trade. They also have enforcement agencies to combat and discourage the practice. The United States, although the activity remains, has a tier one rating for its verified resources and legislation directed towards prosecution and elimination of trafficking.

Countries such as Albania, Belarus, and Greece continue to have tier ratings of three. Mainly they are transit states where trafficked people are held temporarily before being shipped to their final destinations. Their physical proximity to countries such as Moldova, Romania, Russia, Ukraine, and Yugoslavia make them an ideal stop over. Given the description of the murdered girls, she hypothesized, and if what Gonzales said was indeed fact, there was a good chance they had been funneled through that area.

Keep an open mind Donner cautioned the detectives. Trafficking is not restricted to that area. The Netherlands, Ireland, Israel, throughout Africa, the Philippines, Mexico, Canada, and the United States. Human trafficking is an international blight. She assured them that not only the FBI, but the State Department along with Interpol was vigilantly engaged in fighting the trade.

Under the legal definition, to be engaged in the crime of human trafficking, there must be process, a means, and a goal. On a dry eraser board she wrote the three words. Under process she listed recruitment, transportation, transferring, harboring, and receiving. Under means she listed threat, coercion, abduction, fraud, deceit, deception, abuse of power. Finally under goal she wrote prostitution, pornography, violence, sexual exploitation, forced labor, involuntary servitude, debt bondage, slavery, and similar practices.

Turning back to face Tidwell and Sawyer she said, "Victim consent for adults is irrelevant if one of these means is employed. For children, consent is irrelevant."

"I'm just a country boy," Tidwell said. "But to me even without the girls being children one of each three categories is present. That fact that they were children makes it that much more atrocious."

"I don't want to give you the wrong idea," she replied. "We are going to pursue this forcefully with all available resources. But I can't promise you we will shut them down. We'd love to. But I can't make you that promise. Currently there are over four hundred ongoing investigations involving human trafficking. Utopia, if that's their real name, is just one more. "

"What about the Canadian company that buys and sells the girls?" Tidwell wanted to know. "Will you be able to shut them down?"

Making a face she shrugged. "Naturally we will alert the Canadian authorities. Again, keep in mind the Canadians tend to be more liberal than the United States. I'm not trying to say they will turn a blind eye, because they won't. I'm just being pragmatic. I don't want you to be disappointed if they don't."

"Well, as a country boy," Tidwell began. "It seems to me that members of this society, if they read the newspapers or watch television, know their members are being murdered three at a time. That would send up a red flag in my mind that maybe things just aren't too safe. Common sense would tell me that they would want to help us find this guy, you know, to stop the bloodshed. They may even know who he is."

"Preservation instinct," she replied. "Their practices would not receive favorable consideration in the justice system. Besides the humiliation of being exposed as a child molester, dealing in the slave trade, having to register as sexual predators, they face long prison sentences. Sexual predators, as you know, don't survive well in jail." She looked at the two detectives. "The press has never made any link between Utopia and the murders. Until you confirmed their existence Utopia, to us, was just a rumor. They may not even be aware their membership is being targeted."

Sawyer covered his mouth and coughed. His physical condition was rapidly deteriorating, his disease advancing. He cleared his throat. "The FBI is better equipped to handle this than we are. That's why we are here. We would like to be kept in the loop if anything should come of it."

Readily agreeing the agent thanked them for their time and ushered them to the door. In the hall outside her office the two men looked at each other and shook their heads. Exchange of information, particularly information from the FBI to local authorities, was a rarity at best. Both doubted they would hear from her again.

Tidwell drove Sawyer to his home in Asheville and said good-bye. Before leaving he informed the former SBI agent that he was scheduled to fly to Louisiana in a couple of days. Sawyer shook his head, mumbled something about being careful around them Cajuns, and then smiled. Turning serious they exchanged reflections on Sawyer's personal situation. Given only another few months by his doctors, Sawyer rejected their suggested regiment of treatment. For an extra few weeks with no assurances as to the quality of life, he declined their debilitating procedures. Mentally he had made peace with himself. Not knowing what to say, Tidwell promised to report every couple of days, said good-bye, watched his friend enter his home, then drove away.

First developed by the French in 1719, the area surrounding the city of Westwego, Louisiana, as is much of the lower delta of the state, is home to numerous swamps and marshes. Connected to the Mississippi River and Bayou Segnette through various canals and an aging system of locks, Westwego was officially founded by the Texas and Pacific Railroad in 1870. The end of the east bound rail line, folklore insists the name came from conductors telling passengers "west we go." Whether the story is accurate or legend no longer matters. Residents take great delight in telling the tale. Travelers take great delight in hearing it.

Important in the transatlantic slave trade for its water frontage and accessibility to large plantations, the city's earliest residents, like the slave traders, depended on the water to make their living. They were fishermen, shrimpers, oystermen, and trappers; all vocations requiring a certain amount of hardness in their practitioners. Nearby plantations flourished. The rich delta soil worked by the unpaid slave labor rewarded owners with financial stability. The largest, Seven Oaks, was known for its plentiful crops of sugar cane. Others like Whitehouse Plantation, Magnolia Lane, and LaBranche were consumed by the ever expanding city limits; an expansion fueled by incorporation. Incorporation was encouraged by increased population; an increase assisted by an unnamed hurricane in 1893 which devastated the fishing village on Cheniere Caminado. Loss of life on the barrier island was significant and most of the survivors, their homes in ruins, moved to the safety of higher ground in Westwego.

Aided by the computer and the telephone, Tidwell accomplished what he could of the preliminary ground work into Caleb Rousseau's childhood. Records were vague. Retrieving a copy of the birth certificate was a triumph. With the assistance of a long standing school board member who loved to talk he was able to acquire what student records remained. The records proved to be the link to the names and address of the legal guardians, Catherine and Cassandra Monocle. The search had been difficult and time consuming. At the time Rousseau was enrolled in school, the home address was on Vic A Pitre Drive. Current tax records listed the sisters as owners. Tidwell decided to start with them.

Parking in front of the two story home with four white columns, Tidwell looked around the neighborhood. There was a sense of familiarity to the area. Years of living in New Orleans afforded ample occasions for exploration. Spurred by his interest in history he made several excursions in and around Westwego. Now, standing in the street next to his rented car, he was sure he had been at the same spot years ago. Protocol obligated him to inform local authorities of his visit. His request for an officer to escort him to the home was, at first, rejected. Only after he revealed he was formerly a local officer did his reception improve. His request was granted.

At the front door Tidwell and the local uniformed officer rang the door bell and waited. On the second ring the door opened. Standing with one hand on the door was a woman attired in a silk bathrobe. Introducing himself and Tidwell, the officer asked if they could come in.

"What's this about?" The woman wanted to know.

"Caleb Rousseau," Tidwell replied.

The name surprised her causing her face to go white. "Caleb? I haven't seen him in twenty-five years," she managed to say.

"May we come in?" The officer repeated his request.

Nodding she stepped backwards allowing them to pass before closing the door. Ushering them into a sitting room, she occupied a queen chair while motioning them to a sofa with carved arms. Taking in the décor Tidwell realized that most of the furnishings were museum quality antiques. Floor to ceiling striped paper adorned the walls. Suspended from the ceiling a chandelier of glass and gold bathed the room in soft light. Large windows were guarded by dark, heavy drapes which met in the center then swayed to the sides where they were tied with gold cording.

"May I ask if you are Catherine or Cassandra?" Tidwell inquired.

"Cassandra," she replied. "Catherine died three years ago. I still haven't gotten over the loss."

"My deepest regrets," Tidwell said. "I really am sorry to hear that. I was hoping to speak with her as well."

"As you can see, that's not possible." Cassandra was at one time a very attractive woman. Looking at her Tidwell could see that the harshness of old age could not entirely mask the beauty of her youth. "What do you want with Caleb?" she asked her voice wintry.

"Do you know where he is?" Tidwell quizzed.

"No. We don't exactly exchange Christmas cards. As I said, I haven't seen him since he left."

"Ms. Monocle, how did you and your sister come to have custody of Caleb?" As he spoke Tidwell removed a notebook from his jacket pocket.

"He was forced on us." She waved a hand through the air. "That mother of his dropped him here then disappeared. I haven't seen her since either. I swear she was a worthless child without benefit of a brain. White trash she was, nothing but white trash. That's all she ever was, God rest her soul."

"She's not alive?" Tidwell asked, writing on his note pad.

"She met an untimely death. She was murdered about ten years ago out in California. I guess God took pity on her and ended her misery." Cassandra shook her head slowly.

"I am sorry." Tidwell looked up from his note taking. "Let's get back to Caleb, okay? Can you tell us what kind of a child he was?"

"Usually quiet I guess. He kept to himself mostly. He spent a lot of time down in the swamps. Lord only knows what he was doing down there. I know I don't."

"Did he have any friends? You know a best buddy or girl friend?"

"Not really. As I said, he kept to himself."

"Did he get into trouble around here?" Tidwell wanted to know.

"Oh please," Cassandra said. "He was a boy, of course he got in trouble. Isn't that what boys do?" She leaned forward. "But not so much you know. We knew how to handle him."

"And when he got in trouble did you punish him?"

Cassandra leaned back. "When it was necessary, yes we punished him. It was the right thing to do."

Tidwell looked at Cassandra Monocle. Her expression was stoic. "Did you and your sister abuse Caleb?" he asked quietly.

Instantly her eyes filled with indignation. Her voice became bitter. "Let me tell you something Detective whatever your name is."

"Tidwell, Detective Aaron Tidwell," he said calmly.

"Let me tell you something Detective Tidwell. There was no abuse. What we did was prepare him for proper manhood. When he lived here he conducted himself appropriately. He was well fed and well clothed. So many children blame their upbringing for their own mistakes. Abused? The very notion is absurd."

Aaron Tidwell clasped his hands and leaned forward. "Ms. Monocle, Caleb has been telling people that he was sexually abused.

He's told people that he was engaged sexually with both you and your sister. Is that the truth or is he lying?"

Cassandra's face flushed with anger. "That boy could always make up such lies. Never could you believe half of what came out of his mouth. He was always cursed with a wild imagination. And besides," she added. "That was a long time ago. There is nothing anyone can do to change the past." Twisting in her seat caused her robe to fall away from her knees and she quickly adjusted it. "What's all this nonsense about the past anyway? What is it that you think Caleb has done?"

"So you are saying that Caleb is lying about the sexual abuse?"

"Please answer my question sir!" Cassandra was emphatic. "What is it that you think Caleb has done?"

Aaron chose his words carefully. "He is a person of interest in an on going investigation. If I can talk to him I might be able to clear everything up. I might be able to help him. But - before I can do that I have to find him."

Monocle looked at him with a perplexed expression. "You know I don't have to talk with you?"

Tidwell nodded. "Yes, I know that and I do appreciate you taking time for me. I've come a long way looking for answers. I was hoping you could provide some."

"What kind of answers?" There was moisture in Cassandra's eyes.

"Was he a mean person?" Aaron asked. "Did he enjoy inflicting pain on others? What about animals? Did he hurt them or kill them? Was he sexually active? Were there any rumors about him forcing himself on females? Answers to those types of questions can give me a better understanding of Caleb and help end this thing."

She looked at the ceiling, the walls, and then finally the drapes. "Those types of questions are frightening Detective. I have lived and seen and read enough to know those types of questions are normally asked out loud when one is suspected of a horrific crime." She paused. Visibly uncomfortable she labored trying to decide what she should divulge.

"His father was a brutal man. In love with himself, that man was, yes sir. And he deceived himself into thinking that everybody else was in love with him also. But what they were was terrified of him. That's why his mother left. She feared for her life. The only smart thing she ever did. The apple doesn't fall far from the tree, now does it? I heard he fathered another child with some white trash bimbo after Caleb's mother left him. Don't know it for sure, but that's what I heard."

"Did you see that inclination in Caleb Ms. Monocle? Brutality, I mean?" Tidwell's voice was hushed and soothing.

Again Cassandra gazed at the walls. Tears seeped from her eyes. "Once," she said. "Only once. He left a couple of days later. Ran off to I don't know where. After that we started locking our doors. We didn't want him back."

Tidwell, the man, had a growing sensation of nausea. Tidwell, the police detective remained patient. "Can you tell me what happened?"

"No. I'd rather not." Cassandra used a hand to wipe her face.

"Please," Tidwell persisted. "I know it may be difficult. I know it will bring back memories you would rather keep buried. But there are twelve dead bodies spread across four states that need justice. Twelve people who can no longer speak for themselves. It's my job to speak for them."

"And you really think Caleb is responsible for their deaths?"

"I think I need to talk with him," Aaron pleaded. Will you help me?"

Monocle shook her head and lowered her chin to her chest.

Tidwell could see the tears again streaming from her closed eyes. "This house has been the host to pillars of the community," she said, her voice low.

"Catherine and I entertained the dignitaries and business people of this town. Spiritual leaders have sat at our table, given blessings of thanks, and eaten our food. Only a handful of outsiders knew what we did when alone. We worked very hard to keep our private affairs private. To everyone else we were and remain respectable members of the community. Those who knew of our private pleasures lined up to join us when we would permit it." She paused, gathering her thoughts.

"We were cursed with over active libidos; I'll admit that, I always have. Yes, a limited amount of accidental sexual contact between Caleb and us did occur. It was never abuse. It was never forced upon him. He misinterpreted the contact as permission to rape us. The last time he wouldn't stop. He went from one to the other then back again. He was possessed by the devil himself. Finally we resisted. He went into a rage and started to strangle Catherine with his bare hands. He was fourteen. Even at that age he had the strength of a grown man. If I hadn't taken a club to his back he would have killed her."

Silence filled the room after Cassandra stopped talking. Tidwell allowed the minutes to pass as she tried to compose herself. "What you did," he finally said, "was a crime. There is no such thing as accidental sexual contact with a child. You were supposed to be there to protect him, not use him for your own gratification."

"It isn't our fault you know," she shot back. "What he's done. That's not the fault of Catherine or me - those twelve innocent people."

Tidwell stood, his eyes glaring at Cassandra Monocle. "I didn't say they were innocent. Only four were innocent. The others were as guilty as you and Catherine. But even guilty victims deserve justice."

"What's going to happen now?" She used the sleeves of the robe to dab her eyes.

Tidwell shook his head. "That's not up to me."

CHAPTER EIGHTEEN

He was brooding. It was nothing specific he could pinpoint. Yes, he was still angered about what occurred in the Wytheville home. His preparations had been hurried, his time limited by outside restrictions. He censured himself endlessly with curses and psychological beatings. Still, he classified the night as successful. Yet a nagging feeling began to surround him. There was an invisible pressure progressively encompassing his being; suffocating his mental capacities. Too much time had elapsed since he experienced total liberation from his yearnings. Attempting to fend off the cravings was as futile as attempting to hold back the waves of an ocean. An hour did not pass without his thoughts' slipping into his fantasizes. A minute did not pass that he did not think of those he left in the four houses. Somehow he failed them. Failed to show them the righteousness of what they preached but failed to practice. He failed to show them attainable peacefulness. Failed! Failed! Failed! The belief he was spiraling towards eternal psychosis was intolerable to contemplate.

He rebuked her for her negligent attention to her body. She responded by acquiescing to his every order. She embarked on a regiment of exercise. Attentiveness to his every whim became her sacred obligation. Her efforts failed to appease. Fault was directed towards her. Perhaps he was tiring of her attributes. Concluding that was the problem he again faulted her. Masking his sentiments in white lies of half truths he drew her deeper into his world; her atonement for her transgressions. Trips to the homes of strangers became more frequent. Sessions became protracted, their detail more scripted. The participants appeared younger, bolder, and more reckless.

The two females at one home were both younger than she. During the tryst she learned one was barely out of her teens, the other not yet of legal age. On another night she had been surprised by the presence of another male. She had had prior knowledge before arriving at previous encounters that would included the exchange of male partners. Nothing was explained in this instance. His presence worried her. But he did nothing but watch. In Georgia he took her to the home of twins whose lust was as unrelenting as his. They took turns with her, then like a rag doll discarded her and turned their attentions to him. Forced from participant to spectator she sulked. No one noticed when she left the room. But she could not bring herself to rebuff his demands.

Saying only his work was responsible he inaugurated overnight absences. She was not without the ability of reasoning. Work was not the offender. Secretly she felt a sense of relief in her provisional seclusion. The nights of her liberation she divided between self pampering and anguished fretfulness. She knew not to question his activities or movements. His returns meant long sessions of love making, his desires more difficult to satisfy.

Despite his declarations she felt she was failing him. Failure would cause her to suffer. In her guilt ridden mental condition she became confused, unable to think for herself and without his day to day regulation she became forgetful. What she forgot would be considered inconsequential to a rational individual. But it was the small things which sparked his anger and unleashed invective verbal battering. Her uneducated and emotional defense to the mistreatment was to submit further to his decadence.

He knew before her that she was pregnant. The knowledge sent him spinning. In his mind he unfolded, then discarded a thousand different possibilities. Who was the father? Their activities compelled the question be asked. Not readily answerable he hurled his anger in her direction. Prevention was her responsibility. Looking at her with disgust he attempted to stay calm, to rationalize what was required. With an escalating voice he outlined the single acceptable course of action; abortion and sterilization. She attempted to protest. Debate would not be allowed. No resistance would be tolerated. His position was unmovable. His position was ultimate. He refrained from saying out loud that after the procedures he would leave and never return. She had betrayed him and for that she must be shunned. Besides, he had been stationary for too long. Too long in the same place meant greater risk of detection. Too long in the same place made him reckless and sloppy. Too long in the same place was an invitation to having his life's work halted. That, he decided, was a cross he could not bear.

Privately he made the necessary arrangements. The procedures would be preformed in Charlotte. Scheduled for the first Friday in October, the three weeks remaining would be used in vengeances against her.

CHAPTER NINETEEN

Where was Caleb Rousseau? Aaron Tidwell wrote the name on a blank sheet of paper. The nationwide BOLO and the release of the artist sketch yielded nothing. Anonymously he moved about the same way he entered and exited the scenes of his crimes - invisible. Did he really exist? He did at one time. His aunt had saved pictures of him in his youth. Those photos were of little help. A young boy in staged artificial poses with forced smiles. The pictures could have easily been of a million different people. Even the tape handed over by Gonzales failed to capture his image. Unambiguous in documenting the Cromwell's final hours, the sole survivor of the evening was inexplicably absent from the frames. North Carolina, Colorado, Arkansas, Virginia. None had any records of a Caleb Rousseau. Neither did Georgia, South Carolina, or Tennessee. The likelihood he was living under an assumed name was the only coherent rational.

Sitting at his desk Tidwell began to rearrange the letters of the name.

ABE ROUSE

ABLE ROSE

ROSS BELCA

CAL ROSE

ROSS LABCA

ROSS BLECA

C. A. ROUSE

He knew it to be a long shot at best. The morning passed as he filled one page and then another with variations of the name. Somewhere, someone knows this guy and where he is, Tidwell told himself. Just as quickly he cautioned his optimism. Several wanted people successful hid in plain sight for years.

At noon the phone took Aaron away from his attempt to decipher the name. Grateful for the interlude he answered on the third ring. The voice on the other end dripped with a southern accent. He stated he was a deputy sheriff in Virginia and had seen the man in the sketch that Tidwell circulated. He went on to explain how he had stopped to render assistance to someone he thought an average motorist with a flat tire. Asking a few questions Tidwell listened to the responses with growing interest. "Do you remember when that was?"

"I'll never forget it," replied the deputy. "It was the night of the Wytheville murders."

"Okay," Tidwell said scowling. "Are you sure it was the same man?"

"Well, that's the rub detective." The deputy sighed loudly through the receiver.

"What do you mean?" Aaron frowned.

"Well, it was cold that night. The man was wearing one of those wool watch caps pulled down over his ears."

"Okay." Tidwell moved his right hand in a circular motion wanting to reach through the phone and drag the words from the deputy's mouth.

"Well, that picture shows the man with a lot of hair. With the watch cap pulled down like it was I can't say with one hundred percent certainty that my guy had all that hair."

"Then why do think it was him?" Already Tidwell was chalking it up to another dead end.

"Eyes don't lie, detective," the deputy said. "I'll never forget the eyes. If your artist is right then that was your man."

"Could you identify him if you saw him again?" Tidwell asked, anticipating a less than positive response.

"Tidwell, there's only two things I'm sure of in this life. One is that someday we all die and the second one is that I can pick that fellow out of any line up with no problem."

Recording the deputy's information Tidwell asked several more questions before thanking him and replacing the phone in its cradle. Could it be another piece of the puzzle falling into place? He filed the information away and returned to the names he had spread over three pages.

Studying his work Tidwell shook his head. Trying to decide which could be plausible and which were, more than probable foolhardy, consumed the afternoon. In desperation he decided to check each one. Picking up the phone he called motor vehicles and requested a check on all the names. Not expecting any results he stood up, stretched, and left for the day.

Stopping first by the Food Lion to pick up a TV dinner and a six pack of beer he drove to his home. In the kitchen he tossed the dinner into the oven, flipped opened a can of beer, and proceeded to take a long swallow. From the window pane his reflection stared back at him. The image made him sigh. He had aged considerably since the Cromwell's were murdered. His hair was a deeper gray. His eyes were ringed with fresh lines of stress. Only to himself did he admit his fatigue and his perpetual weariness. Only to himself did he acknowledge doubt of ever solving the case.

Deprived of more than sleep he questioned if the outcome would be worth the sacrifices. The relationship between him and his wife had grown increasingly strained as the months passed. Seeking refuge from the tensions within their home, his wife took frequent trips to see relatives; the periods of her absences growing longer with each visit. Aaron reacted to the separations by self-enslavement to his job. But he knew that was ironic.

Soon he could be unemployed. The elections were less than six weeks away. The possibility had been verbalized on several occasions and, at first, the prospects of being relieved of his job depressed him. He owed it to the Cromwell's and to the other victims to bring their killer to justice. In the end wasn't that all that mattered? He knew he was deceiving himself. Yes it was important to remove a menace from the streets. Yes it was important to close the case with a conviction. But now, standing in his kitchen he admitted to himself that other things mattered as well. Perhaps being fired would be a blessing. Unemployment would provide the time to mend fences in his own home; figuratively and literally.

The stove's timer and his pager sounded at the same time. Using a towel as an oven mitt he removed the dinner from the oven and sat it on top of the stove. Looking at the pager he picked up the phone and punched in the number. "This is Tidwell," he responded when the phone was answered. He listened quietly. Saying thank you, he hung up.

Popping the tab of another beer he raised the can in a toast. "I've got you," he said quietly. "I've got you."

Quietly he ate his dinner then went to bed. The date was September twenty-fifth - his birthday. It had been nearly two years since the

Sunday morning discovery of the bodies. Aaron Tidwell celebrated turning fifty by falling into a deep sleep.

CHAPTER TWENTY

September twenty-sixth was a busy day. Rising early Tidwell was in the office before five. Waiting for him was a photo copy of a driver's license picture. "Thank you," he said to no one in particular. Gathering his evidence and information he waited at the state's attorney office. Just before eight an assistant states attorney unlocked the doors and ushered Tidwell in. Hearing the explanation for the unannounced visit prompted the assistant into action. Immediately he was on the phone. As county clerks filtered in they were inundated with orders before they could remove their coats. Sequestering Tidwell in a private office the assistant left the detective to amuse himself as he hovered around the desks of his subordinates. Impatiently Tidwell chewed an unlit cigar. Periodically the assistant state attorney appeared in the room with guarantees that the wait would soon be over. Behind the cigar Tidwell mumbled his responses. Finally, with a grand gesture the assistant announced the arrival of the state's attorney. Motioning for Tidwell to follow, he led him to an inner office and seated him in front of the massive walnut desk.

While presenting his case Aaron was briefly interrupted by periodic questions. "Circumstantial at best," was the State's Attorney's assessment.

"Signed affidavit by Gonzales," Tidwell responded.

The State's Attorney sneered. "Possible co-conspirator and you know it."

"His statement has checked out. There is no reason not to believe him. At the least it's enough for probable cause." Tidwell argued, pushing for an answer.

"It's still weak." Shrugging his shoulders the county's top prosecutor relented. "It's enough to get you your warrants, though. You better find something at the house, Detective. I need more than what you've shown me for a conviction."

The language of the warrants was intentionally vague. With the generalizations and lack of specificity anything from the home could be seized. The warrants amounted to nothing less than a legalized fishing expedition. "Now all you have to do is have a judge sign them. Go see Judge Russell."

Tidwell, saying thank you, hurriedly departed.

Judge Steven Russell was Tidwell's senior by twenty-five years. Tall, thin, silver haired, Judge Russell heard civil cases in the district court. Reluctant to affix his signature for warrants in a criminal proceeding he vacillated over the verbiage. Being as respectful as possible but stressing the urgency of the situation Tidwell talked for an hour, knocking aside each of the judge's objections. Finally Russell agreed to sign. Mindful of the judge's political standing Tidwell was more than enthusiastic in voicing his appreciation.

To notify then assemble an assault team consumed even more precious time. Joe Sawyer and Chet Springs were called. Sawyer declined the invitation to accompany the arrest team, his worsening health rapidly debilitating his body. Springs was in Greensboro investigating another case. Hearing of the warrants he hurried to his car and headed west, promising to be there by early afternoon. It was determined the County SWAT team would provide cover and make the initial entry into the house. The state would supervise closing and sealing all roads with access to the house. Remembering that Alberto Gonzales implied Rousseau would not be taken alive, Tidwell arranged for an ambulance and paramedic team to accompany the small army he intended to gather. Briefed on each and every detail the Sheriff, after weighing political repercussions if events went badly, declined the opportunity to make the arrest.

Springs, slowed by traffic, finally arrived a few minutes after three. The task force briefing started at three-thirty. Standing in front of the sixty officers Tidwell outlined the plan. At the conclusion he answered questions. Emphasizing that they wanted the suspect alive, he cautioned everyone to exercise control. "But," he added. "I don't want any of you hurt. Be careful, but be safe. Understood?"

At four-thirty the caravan of marked and unmarked cars pulled away from the staging area. The vanguard consisted of two state patrol cruisers, the SWAT truck, and Tidwell's unmarked car. Behind them twenty other cars followed. The ambulance was last in line. All traveled without benefit of sirens or flashing lights. Still, a large column of official vehicles was an abnormal site on the lightly traveled roads. Their presence evoked perplexed gawks from even the most indifferent onlookers. As they snaked through the foot hills of the Smokey Mountains Tidwell and Springs refrained from conversation. Both were engaged in the private reflections of a hunter closing in on the prey. Mundane discourse was needless. Slipping past the rising terrain both felt a sense of calm.

The first two cars drove three miles past the lane leading to the house. At that point they flipped on their overhead lights and blocked the road. The SWAT truck pulled into the lane and stopped. From its rear twelve men wearing combat fatigues, bullet proof vests, radio transmitters, and armed with automatic weapons emerged. Dividing themselves into two teams they separated, disappearing into the trees which lined both sides of the lane. Using the tall pines as concealment they traversed the half mile towards the house. B Team would circle the house and cover the rear while A Team would force entry at the front.

Tidwell stopped his car midway up the lane to wait for SWAT to reach their positions. Behind him the lane became choked with stopped vehicles. The ambulance was instructed to remain on the asphalt road until needed. Everyone waited. Three miles before the entrance to the lane the last two patrol cars mimicked the actions of the first two and blocked the roadway. The minutes ticked away. The occasional radio transmissions from team A to team B supplied muffled progress reports. Through the open window of his cruiser Aaron Tidwell smelled the fragrance of fall. Under normal circumstances he would have breathed in the scent with appreciation for the season. But now, waiting impatiently to finish what started months before he felt tense and struggled to fight the urge to speed up the lane and charge the front door.

Wooded mountainous areas are alive with sounds. The wind massaged singing of dancing branches, the crackling of dried leaves as birds hop along the ground, the chattering of squirrels, and the cries of hawks. They are the sounds of peacefulness. They are the sounds of tranquility alerting everyone that all things are right. The unexpected barking of dogs shattered that peacefulness. The element of surprise was lost.

A burst from an automatic weapon silenced the barking as unexpectedly as it had begun. Immediately a radio transmission set the task force in motion. Racing the vehicle up the lane, throwing up a wave of dirt and stone, Tidwell came to a jarring stop in front of the house. Springs leapt from the car, weapon drawn, before Tidwell maneuvered the transmission into park. Members of the SWAT team rushed the steps of the porch, weapons poised, safeties off. The clearing in front of the house was inundated with vehicles and armed officers.

Events became distorted in the fog of attack. SWAT banged loudly on the door while shouting, "Police, open up now!" They were screaming. Tidwell, not waiting for a response motioned for them to go. He too was shouting. The portable battering ram smashed the door open. Or was it simultaneously being opened from the inside. Afterwards it would depend on who was relating the story. All agreed the door tackled the small woman with enough force to knock her to the floor. Her screams drifted into oblivion, drowned in the shouts of the officers. In pain from the impact the woman lay sobbing. Her cries were ignored. Officers pinned her against the floor with weapon barrels and profane commands to stay down.

The blitz flooded every room. The word "Clear!" was shouted, its echo penetrating the chaos. Room by room the team methodically and quickly searched the house. Each room was occupied with uniformed officers. The female escalated to hysteria. Screams mixed with shouted obscenities.

"He's running!" The blaring radio transmission sent Tidwell and Springs hurrying pell-mell out the back door. They cleared the steps of the deck in a single leap. The uphill terrain they faced was rocky and littered with small scrub pines. A foot pursuit would be difficult.

"Police! - Stop!" Tidwell screamed at the fleeing man.

The command slowed him. He turned to look backwards. The look prevented him from seeing the charging officer in his front. A football style waist high tackle by the SWAT member sent them both rolling towards the pursuing detectives. Within seconds the pair was surrounded. Continued resistance was crushed by the weight of bodies.

Handcuffed, searched, and hauled to his feet, Tidwell stood before him. "Are you C. B. Ross?" Instead of an answer Tidwell was greeted with a stare from deep penetrating blue eyes. "Is your real name Caleb Rousseau?" There was another stare from the eyes. "I have a warrant for your arrest. I also have a warrant to search your house, your vehicle, and a warrant to search your person. Do you understand?"

Turning to Chet Springs Tidwell said, "Read him his rights."

Retrieving a card from his jacket pocket Springs read verbatim. When he was finished he asked, "Do you understand these rights as I have explained them to you?"

Transferring his stare from Tidwell to Springs, Rousseau spoke in an emotionless voice. "You can all go to hell; I'm not saying anything without an attorney."

The detectives nodded to one another. They had taken him into custody but they would not be allowed to question him. Taking positions on either side of their prisoner they grasped his arms and walked him around the house to their car. It was finished.

After assisting the prisoner into the back seat Chet slid in next to him. Tidwell took a moment to survey the body of armed officers before sliding in behind the wheel. Starting the engine he looked in the rearview mirror at Rousseau. As the car's motor roared to life he studied the profile of his suspect. For months he wondered what he would feel when he would finally be able to look the murderer in the eye. Would it be the peacefulness of closure? Or would his feelings continue to be those of contempt and hatred? Now, looking through the car's mirror he experienced neither. How strange, he thought. There was nothing. Shifting the transmission into drive he inched his way through the sea of cars.

Other than the three pit bulls SWAT killed no one had been injured. Throwing a cigar into his mouth Tidwell rolled it between his teeth as he made his way down the lane onto the blacktop. Thunder rumbled in the distance and a light drizzle dotted the windshield. All signs pointed to it being a wonderful fall. It had been nearly two years since Aaron Tidwell allowed himself to pay attention to the weather or anything other than the case.

Despite the attempt at secrecy, word of the arrest leaked. Spreading across the county the story miraculously reached every reporter. Arriving at the jail the trio was greeted by camera flashes combined with a chorus of shouted questions. Inching the car through the throng of bodies, Tidwell parked as close to the door as possible. Circling around in front of the vehicle he opened the rear door allowing Springs to exit. Together they reached in and assisted their prisoner as he stepped into the flood of lights and voices. The media did not intimidate Rousseau. Indifferent to their presence he silently returned their stares. Pushing through the sea of correspondents they re-gained privacy once inside the door.

Comprehension of the significance and enormity of the arrest had most on duty deputies standing in wait behind the thick metal door. As Tidwell and Springs ushered Rousseau in and out of hallways and cubicles, impulsive applause erupted. Transferring custody to the booking officers, Tidwell felt a wave of exhaustion wash over him. At that moment all he wanted to do was sleep. Always the consummate politician, the Sheriff had other plans for his lead detective. Suddenly appearing between Chet and Aaron he patted Tidwell on the back. He had scheduled a press conference and ordered his most famous detective to appear. Springs would represent the SBI. Requesting permission to be absent was of no use. The county, meaning the voters, wanted their newest hero visible the Sheriff reminded him. The biggest, most important case in county history demanded the presence of the men who solved it. Nothing else would be acceptable. It was scheduled to begin in twenty minutes. Looking at each other with expressions of disgust, Springs and Tidwell were forced to wait.

As they stepped from the building the lights were blinding. Taking their positions to the rear of the Sheriff, the detectives listened as he addressed the reporters. When finished, a hundred questions were shouted into the air and mingled together. Unable to decipher any one question the Sheriff held up his hands for silence. When that failed to bring control he shouted them down. With order restored he stepped aside and motioned Tidwell to the microphone. Moving forward Tidwell positioned his hands on either side of the makeshift podium. Nodding to a local reporter he waited for the onslaught.

"Are you positive you have the killer?" the reporter asked.

"We believe we do," answered Tidwell.

"One follow-up," the reporter said. Tidwell nodded. "Is your case strong enough to ensure a conviction?"

"Only the courts and a jury can answer that." Looking around the throng Tidwell pointed to another.

"Is the suspect assisting, or cooperating with you at this time?"

"Not at this time," said Tidwell. "We've only had him in custody for less than an hour."

"So he has not confessed?"

"Not at this time." Tidwell motioned to the anchor of the local CBS station.

"Has he said anything?" The question was barely audible.

"He was informed of his rights and his right to counsel. He has chosen not to speak with us without an attorney being present" Exhaustion was creeping into Tidwell's voice and he turned his face to yawn. All he wanted to do was sleep.

"Has one been assigned?"

Tidwell shook his head. "That's a function of the courts, not law enforcement."

"So you have not interrogated him yet? Is that correct?"

"Not at this point. As I stated earlier, the suspect was read his rights and at that point he requested an attorney. As of right now we do not know if we will ever speak with him. That's his right and everyone's right under the constitution."

"What was found at the suspect's home? Did you find anything of value?"

Again Tidwell shook his head. "The property is still being examined by other members of law enforcement. The search warrants were served at the time of the arrest and the warrants are now being executed. Let me remind everyone that the investigation continues. This is not the end but hopefully the beginning of the end."

"How many charges have been made against the suspect?" Tidwell's control over whose turn it was to ask a question disappeared and he resorted to answering those he heard.

"Multiple," he said. "The charges will be read in court."

"Detective Tidwell," a reporter shouted until quieting the others. "Can you say for sure that our two year nightmare of looking over our shoulder, not trusting our neighbors and double locking our doors at night is over? Can you say for residents of Jackson County, and the rest of the country for that matter, that that nightmare is over?"

Tidwell was finished "Let me say this, and this will be the last question. There is still a lot of work to be done tonight. Based on the evidence we now have, this department is confident that we have the right person in custody. Again I say the courts will have the final say, not law enforcement. But let me also remind everyone - locking your doors at night is a practical habit everyone should have." Turning his back to the crowd he joined Springs and entered the building.

Opening the door of his house after midnight, Tidwell was greeted by a ringing phone. The voice on the other end belonged to his wife.

"I saw you on television. You look tired," she said. "But congratulations. I know how much this means to you."

"Well, it's been a long haul, you know," he answered. "How much longer are you going to be away?"

"Maybe a couple weeks I think." She paused. "We need this time. We talked about it before I left."

"You talked about it," he told her. "I'm not sure I participated in the conversation."

"Get some rest," she instructed. "You're showing your age Aaron."

"Everyone does in time. That's our prize for growing older. Youth has always been wasted on the young."

CHAPTER TWENTY-ONE

Eck Waterston went through childhood being teased about his name. For young people the attraction of mocking anything out of the ordinary is irresistible. Eck became Heck, was pronounced Eek, and was manifested into Leek, Week, and Reek. Not affected by the teasing Eck went on to become the face of the public defender's office in Jackson County. In his late fifties, tall, brown eyed, with grey hair once blonde, he had practiced law for thirty years. Around the courtroom Eck was considered a noted litigator who could have reaped financial rewards as a big city attorney. Instead he opted to spend his career defending the poor. His decision to defend the poor, whether the consequence of his adolescent teasing or not, had not made him popular with the victims of crime. Nonetheless, his skill won him the respect of his fellow attorneys. Walking in to meet Caleb Rousseau, Waterston was more than a little apprehensive.

"My name is Eck Waterston," he said introducing himself. "I have been assigned the task of defending you in a court of law." He sat down without offering to shake hands. When seated he produced a yellow pad from his attaché case then stared into the eyes of the man sitting across from him.

Caleb Rousseau, a.k.a. C. B. Ross, stared back. Handcuffed to the table, shackled to the floor, the prisoner maintained his supercilious posturing. When standing he was average in height, shorter than Waterston, but muscled, his body void of unnecessary fat. His head and face were shaven. No tattoos were visible on the exposed portions of his arms and hands. What made him different from the hundreds of other county inmates Waterston interviewed were the eyes. Deep bottomless pools of the coldest blue he had every seen. Looking into them for more than a moment caused a sense of trepidation. Feeling a chill steal down his spine, Waterston got the impression he was looking into the depths of hell.

"Do you understand the situation you are in?" Waterston asked.

For several moments Rousseau didn't reply but continued his piercing glare, taking stock of the man seated across from him. Finally he nodded. "I'm in jail handcuffed to a table. That's my situation." His voice was quiet and calm as if he was not accused of multiple murders.

Waterston let his pen fall from his fingers. "Let's get started on the right foot if we may. You're charged with three counts of first degree homicide, three counts of sexual assault, three counts of sexual assault on a minor, one count of arson with intent to conceal a crime, one count of breaking and entering, and one count of resisting arrest. There are a dozen more they are likely to throw at you, but those are irrelevant. The first ones will get you the death penalty if convicted. That's the situation I am referring to. Not if you're handcuffed to a damn table!"

Rousseau's expression did not alter. "I know my situation."

"Then let's drop the macho bull shit. Everyone in this county, probably this state, wants your life. Everyone! I am the only chance you have. Don't misunderstand me. I am not your friend. I am your attorney. And as your attorney I will make sure you receive the best possible defense. Do we understand each other?"

"Yeah, we understand each other." Rousseau rattled the chains that secured his hands to the table.

"Okay." Waterston picked up his pen. "Since you were not represented at the arraignment, a not guilty plea on all charges has been entered for you by the judge. Bail will be out of the question. Naturally we will file a motion for bail, but you don't have a chance of getting it. We've just begun the discovery process. That will consume months. So an actual trial date is realistically some time next year. My guess would be sometime during the summer."

"And I get to sit in jail until then." Rousseau shook his head. "Bail is a constitutional right."

"It's also at the judge's discretion. The court perceives you as a flight risk. Are they wrong?"

Rousseau offered a tight lipped half grin. "Everyone's a flight risk counselor. There are fugitives in every state and every country. Why would I be different?"

"Besides," Waterston added. "You are safer in here than you would be walking the streets." He paused. "Now, will your wife support your alibi?"

"Sophia?" He shrugged. "She will do what she's told."

"Tell me about your relationship with her. Good? Bad? Is the marriage in trouble, about to break up? Tell me."

"What difference does that make?" Rousseau wanted to know.

"Supportive wife, loving marriage - that makes for a better public perception than say a wife beater who cheats on his wife. You don't beat her do you?"

"She'll do what she's told," Rousseau repeated. "She always has."

"Tell me about Alberto Gonzales. You know who he is, right?" Waterston asked.

"Yeah, I know AG." Rousseau shook his head. "You got a cigarette?"

"I don't smoke," Waterston said. "Do you need cigarettes?"

"Yeah, I could use some."

"Alberto Gonzales?" Waterston returned to the question. "Who is he?"

Rousseau again nodded. "He's a punk that thought he could kick my ass. He spent a couple of weeks in the hospital realizing he was wrong. It gave him time to rethink his attitude. I haven't seen him in years. I didn't even think he'd be alive now."

"Why's that?"

"AIDS, that's why. As I said, he's a punk, a man whore. He'd bed anything, male, female, or shemale. He didn't care. And if that didn't do it I figured he would piss someone off enough where they would kill him. He had a knack at doing that. Pissing people off, I mean."

"He says you sent him a video of the Cromwell's murder. He traded it for life imprisonment instead of the death penalty."

Rousseau laughed a low guttural laugh. "Yeah, what did he do?"

"He killed a cop. You didn't know?" Waterston was surprised as Rousseau shook his head no. "Did you send him the video?"

Rousseau's smile and laugh vanished. Suddenly he was all business. "Does this video show me?"

"I haven't seen it yet. I have been told it is of the Cromwell murders." Waterston looked at his client. "Are you saying that you are not in the video or that you did not send it to Gonzales?"

"You see me on the video," Rousseau said, "And I'll save everybody a headache and plead guilty. If you don't then I'm not guilty and you get me out of here."

"Did you know the Cromwell's?" Waterston changed courses.

"Yeah I knew who they were." Rousseau's smile returned. "I know a lot of people. I read the papers. Hell, everybody knows who they were."

"Did you ever have personal contact with them? Were you ever in their home? Did you ever have any sexual contact with them?" Waterston's questions went unanswered. "Did you rape them?"

"They were some lookers weren't they?" For a split second Rousseau's eyes lost some of their hardness. "Nothing is more pleasing to the eye than a good-looking woman, more pleasing to the spirit than the company of one. You know who said that counselor?"

Waterston shrugged. "No, I don't."

"Franklin Roosevelt. Even the cripple he was, he still thought about it. Yeah, the Cromwell women were very pleasing to the eye - even mine. But that's not a crime. And even if I jerked off thinking about them, well, that's not a crime either. You know I could really use that cigarette."

Waterston sat quietly for a few moments. His client had neither confessed nor denied the charges against him. For whatever reason, Rousseau remained indifferent to the seriousness of the circumstances. Rising slowly he went to the door, pounded, and waited until it was open. In whispers he spoke with the guard then returned to his seat. "Okay, Mr. Rousseau, let's go over everything."

"What about my cigarettes?" Rousseau wanted to know.

"The guards are seeing what they can do," Waterston said. Rousseau snickered, doubting the guards would care whether he had cigarettes or not. "Tell me about you. What do you do and where you have been for the past six years? Have you ever lived in Arkansas?"

"Yeah, I lived in Arkansas once. I didn't like it much." With only the slightest of prodding Rousseau launched into his life's story.

He spoke softly but rapidly and Waterston strained to distinguish the separate words. As Caleb spoke Eck observed that, like most people, he enjoyed talking about himself. Unashamed he spoke of his connections in the adult entertainment world. It was there he met Gonzales. Through false modesty he refrained from detailing his sexual conquests but emphasized his services on certain film sets was more than welcome. Savoring the telling of days past did nothing to soften the blank expressions of his eyes. If he hadn't witnessed the rare flicker of softness Waterston would have assumed they never changed.

Casually Rousseau spoke about meeting his wife and how he was swept off his feet. She had, he said, as the saying goes, changed his ways. Waterston doubted the truthfulness of the statement.

With the same matter of fact speech he used when speaking about his wife he related their frequent moves. Reciting from memory the exact dates of their relocations he offered no explanations for their necessity, nor excuses for his lack of explanation. His verbiage, combined with his presentation, was nothing more than the recitation of fact. The only visible emotion he displayed was when speaking of his dogs that were shot. He concluded with his arrest and incarceration.

Waterston listened vigilantly. He watched Rousseau's body language for tell-tale signs of emotions or feelings. He watched the facial expressions for hints of joy, grief, sadness, or concern. None were forthcoming. At last he was forced to conclude he was in the presence of someone totally void of emotion. Within everyone he defended there was always some trace of emotion. Most times his clients would display anger, or hatred, or fear and some would display sadness. But regardless of which emotion their feelings were genuine.

His willingness to defend them was rooted in his belief that there is a little good in all things bad and a little bad in all things good. He could not say the same for his new client. All children are born sinless, without prejudice of any kind, and blessed with an abundance of purity. That purity is eroded through life. Exposure to parental nurturing, circumstances, and environment influences prejudices. Biblically speaking every human is guilty of sin. Yet, even through the trials of life a certain amount of purity is retained in the soul. But in Rousseau there was a distinct and noticeable absence of purity. Perhaps it had been burned away by the flames of fated damnation. Perhaps Rousseau was one in a billion whose birth was cursed by the ill winds that rob a soul of humanity. Or perhaps Caleb Rousseau was the child of the Devil. Whichever the case Waterston acknowledged to himself he would be grateful when no longer forced to be in close proximity to his client.

"From what I know right now, other than the tape," Waterston said, "the state's case is very circumstantial. Naturally we will know more as time progresses. I'll be speaking with your wife."

"Is that really necessary?" Rousseau asked. The thought seemed to annoy him.

"Yes," Waterston stated. "We need her to corroborate you being home the night of the murders. We also need her to corroborate everything you've told me. Is there anything you would like me to tell her?"

"She'll do what you tell her," Rousseau answered. "She always does."

"I'm not going to tell her anything. I want her to tell me." Waterston packed his attaché case. "One last thing, I think it wiser not to make any statement to the police." Rousseau nodded his agreement. "And do yourself a favor by not talking to the other inmates. Sometimes the authorities will put an informer in the same cell as the person their trying to convict." He paused as he stood. "From what I've seen today, I don't think you will have a hard time keeping your mouth shut."

CHAPTER TWENTY-TWO

Sophia went by the name Ross. It was the only name she used since she and Caleb had been together. She was a small woman whose recent lack of sleep affected her facial appearance causing her to look older than her twenty-two years. Under normal conditions she would be described as attractive. Fading freckles dotting each cheek were now highlighted by the lack of mascara. Her hazel green eyes were puffed from her tears. Underlined by the emerging lines induced by stress, they had begun to lose their normal twinkle. Her long reddish hair was uncombed. Hanging lifeless on her thin shoulders it appeared unwashed and matted. An ill fitting sweater and sweat pants camouflaged the softness of her figure. Seated in her living room, between bouts of weeping, she attempted to answer Eck Waterston's questions.

The house they sat in was ordinary, typical for members of the working class. With used furniture of varying degrees of comfort it was not unlike many homes the attorney visited to interview families of the accused. Clean and neat, yet teetering on poverty, the home, like its occupants, attracted no second look. As they spoke Waterston found Sophia to be naïve, uneducated, but believable. Repeatedly she stated she would say anything he wanted. Repeatedly he reminded her he was there to gather information not to influence what she said.

She couldn't remember the night the Cromwell's died, but, she added quickly, she was positive Caleb had been with her. She insisted they were together every night.

"Your husband says you moved frequently. Can you tell me why?"

Using a shredded tissue she wiped at her eyes. "No reason I don't suppose. He just gets restless, you know. He jokes about it and says he's part gypsy." Sophia's smile was forced and not convincing.

Waterston had a hard time imagining Caleb having a sense of humor. "Tell me about the night the police came and took your husband away. What can you tell me about that night?"

She lowered her head as tears dripped down her face. "Just all of a sudden they were here. The dogs were going crazy and Caleb went out back to see what was upsetting them. That's when we heard the shots. You know they killed our dogs?" She looked up in Eck's direction. He nodded. "Those dogs wouldn't hurt anyone," she continued. "They were just pups. It ain't right you know? Them killing them dogs. It just ain't right."

"What happened next?" Waterston asked.

"They was banging on the door and hollering. I was trying to open it when they broke it open. They pushed me to the floor and came runin' in, going in every room, yelling at me to stay on the floor, pointing guns at me. Are they allowed to do that Mr.Waterston? I mean, treat people like that in their own home?"

"They do it for their protection," Waterston explained. "They weren't angry with you. They just wanted to be safe." He wiped his face with his right hand. "Where was your husband at the time the police entered?"

Sophia pointed to the back of the house. "He'd gone out back to see about the dogs. He wasn't trying to run away like they say he was. He wanted to check on the dogs."

"What happened after they arrested Caleb and took him away?" Waterston's question sent Sophia into another stint of sobbing.

"After that all the others came in," she said while wiping her eyes.

"What others?"

"The other cops, but they weren't carrying guns," she answered, her arms waving in every direction. "They were just tearing through everything, opening all the drawers and cabinets, putting stuff in plastic bags and all, and then I went out on the porch and I saw more out in the barn. I guess they were doing the same thing out there."

"Can you tell me what they took with them?" Eck asked as he wrote on his legal pad.

"I'm not really sure of everything they took. I know they took his guns."

Her crying subsided but the memory of the house being searched ignited a flicker of anger. The anger trickled into her voice.

"Now this is important," Waterston said leaning towards her. "What type of guns?"

"I don't know anything about guns. There were a couple of pistols and his shotguns. Are they allowed to do that, just steal someone's property?"

"It's not really stealing Sophia," Waterston said. "The court told them they could take anything they believe to be evidence. What else did they take?"

She waved her hand across her face as if swatting an unseen pest. "Movies and pictures, you know that sort of thing."

"What kind of movies?" Waterston's mind thought of the tape sent to Alberto Gonzales. For the police to find a copy of it in Rousseau's home would mean a guaranteed conviction.

Sophia lowered her head hiding her eyes. "They were sex movies. We only have a few but Caleb liked to watch them. He said it wasn't against the law. Is that right? And, do we get those back?"

"Perhaps," Waterston stated. "As long as they are legal. What were the pictures of?"

"Nothing special, really." Sophia tucked her legs under her and shifted in the chair to get comfortable. "Just pictures of me naked. Caleb says lots of men have naked pictures of their wives. Is that true?"

"I suppose it could be." Clearing his throat Waterston asked for a glass of water. As Sophia rose to go to the kitchen her sweater suddenly drooped revealing bruises below the base of her neck. When she returned with the water he drained the glass before continuing.

"Did Caleb ever beat you?" he asked.

"What!" Sophia's voice filled with shock and confusion.

"I know this is difficult, but I have to ask. Is Caleb a good husband?"

"Of course he is." Her flood of tears returned. "Caleb wouldn't hurt me. He wouldn't hurt anybody unless they needed it. We love each other."

"I'm sorry," Waterston said apologetically. "But when you stood up I saw the bruises. I had to ask."

Instinctively she grabbed the neck of the sweater clutching it closed. "Caleb didn't do that," Sophia sobbed. "The police did that when they knocked me to the floor."

"Again I'm sorry." For a moment Eck flipped the pages of the legal pad as if looking for a specific item. "What do you and Caleb do together for fun? You know, that makes you both happy?"

"We don't really do anything special." Sophia shifted her eyes skyward as she thought. "No hobbies or things like that. We spend a lot of time in the bedroom…" she paused briefly. "Caleb likes it when we're together with no clothes on and all and I kind of like it to. So I guess you could say we like to fuck for fun." She said the words without any thought of their acceptability, with no attempt to shock, or use of the word as an expletive. There was no anger or unfriendliness in the word. She had been asked a question and she responded with childlike truthfulness. No regrets or emotions. Automatically Waterston knew it would be risky to put her on the witness stand.

"Mr. Waterston," she said. "Can I ask you a question?" With her tissue in tatters Sophia wiped her eyes with the sleeve of her sweater.

"Of course," he said.

"Well, with Caleb in jail and all, who is going to take care of me? I mean, Caleb worked, made money, paid the bills, he bought me stuff, and he took me to the store. Now I don't have anybody doing that. And with me being pregnant what's going to happen to me?" Throughout their time together she relegated outside contact to her husband. Without appropriate guidance she was unprepared for independent living.

"Do you have family near by?" Waterston knew she didn't but asked anyway. She shook her head no. "Have you asked for help from the county or the state? You know there are agencies that can help you."

"I don't drive and the police took our car anyway," she said "Will I get that back?"

"Perhaps in time," he answered. "In the meantime I can arrange for you to get to town to apply for social services. Do you have any money?" Sophia shook her head. "What about church members? Do you belong to a church?" Again she shook her head no. "Okay. When I get back to my office I'll make some phone calls and see what I can do. For now," he reached into his pocket and pulled out a few folded bills. "It isn't much but it might help a little."

Timidly she reached out and took the money.

As much as the Cromwell's were victims, Sophia Ross was also a victim. The difference was the lack of an advocate. The state would work conscientiously to ensure the Cromwell family received justice. No one would care that Sophia had also been victimized by the alleged actions of her husband. Innocent of any wrong doing or maliciousness except being married to a suspect, her plight and poverty would mainly go ignored. She would join the ranks of thousands before whose worlds were shattered. She would be shunned because of her daily association with her spouse, and left with few opportunities. Public perception always leaned towards that of the spouse having prior knowledge of the criminal activity. In Waterston's experiences that conjecture was, for the most part erroneous. It was the part of society he disdained.

CHAPTER TWENTY-THREE

Grand jury's have a single responsibility - the determination of sufficient probable cause to return an indictment. But in their secret closed door proceedings no judge sits at the bench as guardian of the rules of evidence or guardian of the accused constitutional rights. Members of a grand jury, unlike those in regular trails, are not screened for biases or other factors which might affect their findings. Targets of grand juries have no rebuttal. Denied access to confront those who accuse them their only remedy is to defend themselves in open court. In theory grand juries are independent entities. Their original purpose was noble; a buffer between over zealous prosecutors and private citizens. Theory is seldom reality. Prosecutors control the process, the presentation of evidence, the questioning of witnesses, and determining what is and what is not relevant. True independent thinking grand juries are rare. Critics argue they have erased their independence to become rubber stamps for prosecutors. Jackson County's prosecutor had no trouble in winning a grand jury indictment against Caleb Rousseau.

Aaron Tidwell's time was now consumed by assisting the prosecutor in preparation for trial. Copying and turning over files was a boring but restful respite from the previous months. Touted a hero, a status he knew had a limited life span, Tidwell approached the holiday season with optimism. His wife returned to North Carolina before Thanksgiving, her presence relaxing the strain on the marriage. Denied time off during the investigation he took advantage of the current atmosphere and scheduled a getaway for the week before Christmas. Both he and his wife were avid history buffs and Aaron arranged a five day trip to Winchester, Virginia.

Originally called Frederick Town, Winchester had its beginnings circa 1729. Burrowed between the Blue Ridge and the Appalachian Mountains the compact city of nearly twenty-five thousand covers a meager nine square miles. Yet within those miles stand thirteen sites on the National Register of Historic Places including George Washington's headquarters circa 1757, the Old Stone Church, circa 1788, and the headquarters of Thomas "Stonewall" Jackson of the Confederate Army. A Mecca for amateur historians and Civil War re-enactments, it is reported the city changed hands during the war over seventy times. At Christmas the city was an amazing display of lights and decorations.

West of Washington D.C. about seventy-five miles, the seasons rapidly changing weather distributed a slight dusting of snow the night the Tidwell's arrived. Inside their room at the bed and breakfast the couple was unconcerned about the flakes of snow. After enjoying a succulent meal at a downtown restaurant they returned to the room to relax and rekindle the pleasures of one another's company. Lying on the bed Aaron read aloud from one of the many brochures they plucked from the front desk.

"Pasty Cline lived here. Did you know that?" Aaron asked.

His wife, unpacking their suitcases laughed. "No. I don't think I did know that."

"Ever hear of Spotswood Poles?" Aaron asked her. She laughed again and shook her head. "He lived here too." He smiled.

"So? Who was he?" she wanted to know.

"A baseball player," Aaron replied. "A Negro baseball player to be exact. He played in the league they had before the Negro league."

"Is he in the Hall of Fame?" she asked, a teasing twinkle in her eye.

"I don't know. I've never been to Cooperstown." He flipped the brochure over. "Doctor Hunter McQuire lived here to. A long time ago though. He was Chief Surgeon for Stonewall Jackson's Second Corps of the Army of Northern Virginia."

"How about that," she said joining him on the bed.

"It says here he helped lay the foundations for future Geneva Conventions regarding treatment of medical doctors during war. That's pretty impressive don't you think?"

Leaning over she kissed his forehead. "What's impressive is that you haven't talked about the job since we left Jackson County."

He compressed his lips. "I really was long over due for a break, you know." What he didn't tell her was that since arresting Rousseau he struggled with an inner emptiness. Instead of feeling elated he felt depressed.

"Do you think?" She slid down the bed snuggling close. "I'm proud of you and happy that it will soon be over."

"I hope so," he responded as his cell phone rang. Looking at the number he cringed. Seeing his face she instantly sat up. Cringing again he ignored the spirited shaking of her head and flipped open the phone. "Tidwell," he mumbled. Listening to the voice on the other end he nodded a few times and before saying good-bye said only "Okay."

Tidwell's wife looked intently at her husband. Her face was twisted with an angry expression. "What," she demanded.

"Joe Sawyer died," Aaron said quietly while tossing the phone on the bed. "The memorial service is the day after we get back."

Her anger evaporated. "I'm sorry. I know you were close."

"He was good man."

The news of Sawyer's passing caused a cloud of sorrow to hang over the remnants of their getaway. Going through the motions of playing tourist, Tidwell spent more time in reflection than entertainment. Trying to savor the time away from his job, he attempted to enhance the days with light hearted conversation and cheerful witticisms. The perfect weather and forced cheer aided his charade of peacefulness.

Driving homeward his mind was weighted with his memories of Joe Sawyer and for most of the trip he didn't speak. Dropping his wife at home with a promise of not being long, Tidwell proceeded to his office. At his desk he flipped through the accumulated mail. Most he ignored. The large white envelope with no return address made him curious and he slid his letter opener quickly through the glued flap. Inside was Joe Sawyer's journal. Bound in soft leather, the faded booked contained Sawyer's thoughts about the investigation they worked together. Briefly he thumbed the pages before turning his attention to the two typewritten pages which accompanied the book.

Tidwell:

Knowing you are away I dared not disturb your much needed time with your wife. For me the end is near. The easy part will be to die. The hard part has been living the past few months. As strange as it may sound, I do look forward to having the rest of eternal sleep. It is my deepest desire that those whom I consider friends find comfort in the knowledge of my peacefulness. But before that appointed hour I must thank you. Unknowingly you have provided me with renewed faith in the goodness of mankind. Surrounded by the wickedness of our occupations your example of integrity and reliability, regardless of personal considerations, can only be founded in the proposition of a patriot in service to his fellow beings. I applaud you, sir. It has been my honor to have known and served with you. That fact alone dictates you retain my journal. It is yours for whatever purpose you deem appropriate.

As you read this I am confident that I have, by this time, expired. As I leave this world I impart to you what little wisdom I gained during my stay in it. Under normal circumstances things are not always as they appear. Under the tragic circumstances our profession births, things are never as they appear. Be not quick to judge, nor slow to act. Remember a mirrored image is always opposite of the truth.

May you grow old, but when your life is over may you be with God before the Devil knows your dead.

J. Sawyer

Folding the letter Tidwell brushed the start of a tear from the corner of his eye. Taking a deep breath he looked up at the ceiling. He could count the number of true friends he had known on one hand. Joe Sawyer was one of them. Placing the letter inside the journal he slipped both into his desk drawer. In the morning he would say good-bye to his friend forever. The thought saddened him. Leaving the office he made his way home. The thought of sharing the letter with his wife never crossed his mind.

The memorial service was a large affair. Flowers dominated the front of the chapel and lined the length of both walls. Uniformed and plainclothes officers from federal, state, county, and local agencies mingled together, filling the sanctuary. Spilling out the double doors they stood on the steps to hear the service. It was the largest tribute Tidwell had witnessed. The chosen orators depicted Joe Sawyer as the good and respected man he was. Enlarged pictures of Sawyer during various stages of his life were hung on the walls for guests to view. Covered with the American flag the casket was kept closed.

When the speeches were completed the six SBI officers in full uniform took their positions as pall-bearers, hoisted the casket, turned, and slowly made their way towards the waiting hearse. More than two hundred vehicles drove the twenty miles to the cemetery. Tidwell, standing in the back of the mourners strained to hear the final words of the minister at the gravesite. The sermon's end led to the firing of the twenty-one gun salute and the bagpipes playing of Taps. The service was complete. Lingering only momentarily at the grave, Tidwell silently said his farewell.

Navigating through stop and go traffic Tidwell crept his way through Asheville heading west towards Jackson County. As city structures gave way to suburb housing and country foliage, he turned on the radio, loosened his tie, and jammed an unlit cigar between his teeth. As he neared Sylva the tones of his cell phone intruded on his reverie and made him jump. Flipping the front of the phone open he answered, "Tidwell here."

"There's been another murder," the Sheriff's voice proclaimed. "You've got the wrong man."

"What?" Tidwell's mind had been deep in memories of Joe Sawyer.

"Another family murdered in their home," the Sheriff said. "Just like all the others. This is on your head Tidwell, you know that don't you; you and those bumbling SBI agents."

As the words penetrated his mind, Tidwell became focused. "Are you sure it's not just a copy cat killing?" he asked the Sheriff.

"Yeah I'm sure," was the reply. "It's the same MO, in fact it was the exact same damn MO!" The Sheriff's voice had risen to just below a shout. "Now I thought we had this bastard locked up! Isn't that what I told everybody? Are you trying to make me look like an idiot?"

A sinking feeling swept over Tidwell. His mind whirled as he searched for logical possibilities. Cursing to himself he asked, "Where?"

"Columbia, South Carolina, that's where. We got the wrong man in fucking jail!" The Sheriff's anger boiled over. "Now get your ass back here! I want a complete explanation!"

"I'll be there in a few minutes," Tidwell said before snapping his cell phone closed.

Driving the last few miles his mind raced outpacing the speed of the car. There was no explanation. Rousseau was in isolation and would be until his court date. There was no way he committed the most recent murders. The media hype since his arrest was staggering. Arkansas, Colorado, and Virginia all filed charges against him for those murders. Only through the legal maneuvering and skillful litigation of his attorney had Rousseau avoided extradition. Regardless of what the Sheriff demanded, Tidwell knew there was no compact explanation that would appease everyone.

Realistically there were only three possibilities. The first and most desired was that the killings were a copy cat. On its face it would be the same but different details, insignificant to casual observers, would prove there was no connection. The second possibility was there were two different killers engaged in a twisted competition. Could there be two killers duplicating the same MO, the same motive, and the same details in every crime? That would be absurd. It would also be terrifying. The final possibility, the one Tidwell prayed would prove incorrect, was that Rousseau was in fact innocent. Remembering the words in Sawyer's letter about nothing being as it appears in tragic circumstances, Tidwell shuddered.

Parking the car he entered the office quietly.

CHAPTER TWENTY-FOUR

Identical in even the smallest detail, the Columbia murders were, without question, the work of the same perpetrator. The singular difference, the proximity of neighboring houses, only added to the frustrations. The killer was growing bolder. The tri-level home yielded no forensic evidence. No finger prints. No witnesses. The mood in law enforcement offices of four states turned sour.

Eck Waterston was anything but sour. In a flurry of activity he filed a motion demanding charges against his client be dismissed. Circumstances dictated Rousseau's release, Waterston argued. With little deliberation the judge agreed. The charges were dismissed. Months after his arrest Caleb Rousseau walked away a free man. Promptly he retained the services of a civil attorney who was more than willing to file a false imprisonment suit against Jackson County.

Local political leaders fumed. Inundated with demands for the Sheriff's removal they attempted to appease their constituents by ordering an independent investigation of his office. Publicly they stated those responsible would be held accountable. Privately they suggested more diplomatic solutions. Their political oratory, intended for public ears, starkly differed from reality. Good old boy etiquette prohibited the removal of the Sheriff. They did not prohibit evaporation of future support for re-election. But the removal of a minion was essential to calm the outcry. Naturally the focus shifted to Detective Aaron Tidwell. His had been the face of the investigation. His would be the face of accountability. Action would be delayed until the conclusion of the independent review. Politics at all levels feeds on scapegoats. Jackson County had, in Aaron Tidwell, the perfect person to sacrifice.

Instantly a pariah to his superiors, Tidwell was ordered to reopen the case. His requests for travel and investigative funds were denied or ignored. Knowing they essentially based his conclusions on the statements of Alberto Gonzales, Tidwell knew it was imperative to question the convict a second time. Daily he requested travel funds. Approval was begrudgingly made. After alerting prison officials, he booked a flight for the day after New Years.

The optimism he had prior to his vacation metamorphosed into anger. He was angered by the damage to his reputation. He was angry at the political cronies tenaciously attempting to offer him in sacrifice, First and foremost he was angry that the killer was still out there. And finally, without understanding why, he was angry at the world. Suspending holiday plans he spent the days riveted to old files.

The dawn of New Year's Eve brought a cold freezing rain across the state of Colorado. Inmates in the state penitentiary, unable to utilize the exercise yard were restricted to the dining hall and their cells. Tensions flared during the noon meal when two inmates scuffled over a particular seat. Sent back to their cells with the threat of a lockdown, the inmates were left to their own devices to pass the remnants of the day.

In block B, Alberto Gonzales, high on contraband coke, spent his time flipping cards against the wall. Snickering in an insidious squeal he rocked to and fro incessantly chanting the same words. "Beelzebub wins! Beelzebub wins! Beelzebub wins!" His cell mate, Roger Hangdon, an arsonist thought to have started over a hundred fires, grew increasing agitated at Gonzales' actions. His demands for Gonzales to stop the illogical chanting were answered with more of the same. "Beelzebub wins! Beelzebub wins!"

Reaching under his mattress Hangdon retrieved the knife he had fashioned from a stolen spoon. Once again he demanded Gonzales to stop.

"Beelzebub wins!" Gonzales chanted again.

In a single swift movement Hangdon was on top of Gonzales his shiv buried to its hilt. Gonzales had no time to scream.

The guards found Gonzales lying in his own blood. Stabbed repeatedly, he bled to death before assistance could arrive. Hangdon sat quietly on his bunk. "He wouldn't shut up," he told the guards. "The dumb shit wouldn't shut up."

The New Year did not portend good things for Aaron Tidwell. The news of Gonzales' death added to his grim disposition. Rejecting invitations for attendance at celebrations he slipped from the old year to the new seated at his desk surrounded by a mountain of files.

There was no place to start except at the beginning. Systematically Tidwell took the case step by step. The transcripts of interviews and affidavits were voluminous and he doggedly read every word. Things are never as they appear. Never as they appear. He repeated the phrase in his mind. Rousseau had appeared guilty. Everyone believed him guilty and yet in the end he was innocent. A mirrored image is always opposite of the truth. Sawyer's words haunted him as much as the glossy pictures staring up from his desk. The opposite of truth and never as they appear. The phrases explode in his brain and he wrestled with himself to find their significance. Remembering Sawyer's journal he sequestered in his drawer he retrieved it and began to read.

He yawned. He read. He yawned. Heavy eyes threatened to deny him sight. Forcibly willing them to respond Tidwell was ready to submit to exhaustion when his eyes focused on a single sentence. Shaking his head he read it a second time. A third reading had him wide awake.

"Christ Almighty!" He shouted obscenities at the empty room. Turning back to the journal he read the sentence out loud. "Lester's LA acquaintances include S. Cummings/A. Gonzales/T. Disher/ G. Reynolds/ F. Pomerleau/ C. Rousseau/ none reside in N. C. and should not be considered persons of interest." Again he shouted curses to no one.

Tidwell's heart raced. Was A. Gonzales Alberto? Was C. Rousseau Caleb? Did the three know each other? Had Lester and Gonzales conspired to frame Rousseau? Rousseau had nearly killed Gonzales, but Gonzales denied his testimony was out of revenge. And what about Lester? Had Rousseau in someway injured him as well? Questions swamped the detectives mind. Why did they fail to make the connection?

Tidwell swallowed deep breaths of the room's stale air endeavoring to slow his thoughts. Lester had an alibi for the Virginia murders; sworn statements from deputies. Did they lie under oath? Joe Sawyer, his journal the only reference linking the three, completely missed the correlation of the names. Had his illness prevented him from comprehensible thought? Jumping to his feet Tidwell disturbed the unstable mass of files on his desk, and sent them to the floor. Their contents scattered across the room. Another harangue of expletives escaped his mouth as he bent down.

It was a hell of a way to start the New Year, Aaron thought as he began the process of restoring order to the clutter. As his eyes surveyed the files on the floor they came to rest on a photograph that somehow isolated itself from the scattered papers. Reaching down he froze, his hand static above the enlarged photo. Slowly he plucked the picture from the floor. Holding it at arms length he ignored the other files. Unaware he was captured on film; David Allen Lester's eyes stared outward, blank and emotionless. Tidwell remembered the feeling of evilness when in his presence. He also remembered the attitude of arrogance that oozed from Lester's every pore. Suddenly Sawyer's letter made sense. A mirrored object is the opposite of the truth. His size, build and appearance were a mirrored image of Caleb Rousseau.

Tidwell started digging through the files he had scattered haphazardly across his desk. Within minutes he extracted what he sought. Holding the two pictures beside each other he gasped. "Holy Christ!" he said. His heart pounded his pause kept pace with his self berating. "Shit!" he yelled. The resemblance was uncanny. He often heard that everyone on earth has a twin but never gave much credence to the theory. Now, if he did not know better he would swear he was looking at brothers.

In person Lester was a little smaller than and not as muscular as Rousseau but the sameness of the eyes was unmistakable. For long minutes Tidwell tormented himself over the possibility that Lester had eluded their detection for months. If true his evasive actions resulted in additional deaths. The media coverage of Rousseau's arrest could only have inflated Lester's enormous sense of superiority, providing the catalyst and opportunity for what was apparently becoming an unappeasable thirst. Lester's ravenous lust foiled the perfect frame. Patience would have seen Rousseau convicted. Patience would have assured the perfect crime. Local sentiment would have assured Rousseau's conviction.

With new energy Tidwell hastily reassembled the scattered files. Concentrating on Sawyer's report from California he dissected every word of the transcripts. No mention of Gonzales or Rousseau. What was missing? Convincing himself he missed the reference he read them again. Finished he rummaged through the papers until he found Lester's interviews. Slowly he probed the pages as if what he thought would be magically displayed in bold highlighted letters. There was nothing.

Nothing, that is, except a reinforced attitude of dislike for Lester. Street hardened criminals would have, to some degree, cracked under the bombardment of questions. Lesser people would have crumbled. Yet at no time did the voice waver from its unnerving calmness. At no time did the face display emotion or discomfort. No sweaty palms no double-crossing beads of perspiration suddenly appearing on the forehead, no lashing out of anger suddenly released.

Twice, three times, ten times he read and re-read the transcripts. As void as the crime scene were of forensic evidence the interviews were equally void of incriminating words. Unswerving denials was the bulk of the interviews. What couldn't be classified as a denial could only be described as placating. Looking at the pictures of the Cromwell's in death failed to rattle Lester. But why should they? If guilty he witnessed it first hand. If guilty he certainly lacked remorse.

Why would the pictures cause him distress? Didn't they have a video of the murders? If guilty he was responsible for recording it.

Still, unanswered questions were more plentiful than certainties. Speculation was useless. A superfluity of unconnected dots, he knew, would plague him if he failed to make the connections. California held the answers. California, he needed to visit. Tidwell knew his superiors would not look with sympathy on another expense. To them he bungled the case from the start with inferior work. The fact that they sent him to Colorado to interview Gonzales was a known but ignored point. The fact they arrived at the same hypothesis from the evidence would be buried by silence. The fact that they wanted him to be their martyr reinforced his determination to prevent it. He would go to California in search of the truth.

But prior to any excursion there were questions that needed answers. Finding the sworn statement of the deputy detailed to watch Lester the night of the Wytheville murders Tidwell called the watch commander. The deputy's presence was required, he explained. The tone of Tidwell's voice indicated the word request was camouflage for the word order.

Deputy Anthony Ohner leisurely made his way past the cubicles to the interrogation room. Instructed to be seated by Tidwell, Ohner complied then folded his forearms on the table which separated him from the detective. Tidwell remained standing.

"We in law enforcement," Tidwell began. "Attempt to dissuade private citizens from making false sworn statements. Usually those statements take the form of an apparition which, in the end, surely comes back to haunt them. Do you know where I'm going with this Deputy Ohner?"

"No," Ohner said seemingly puzzled. "I really don't."

"You really don't?" Tidwell asked incredulously as he seated himself. "Are you sure about that?"

Removing his arms from the table Ohner leaned backwards balancing the chair on the two back legs. "I haven't got a clue to what you're talking about Detective," he said.

"Have you ever made a false statement then sworn to it?" Tidwell's voice was serene. "You know a little white lie that really doesn't hurt anyone. In fact when you say it you think you are protecting someone you don't want to get hurt. That kind of false statement; did you ever make one?"

"Of course not, I'm a cop." Ohner returned the chair to all four legs. "Listen detective, if you've got something to say then just say it and stop the twenty questions routine." A three year veteran of the department Ohner's record was unsullied by complaints, and he was prideful of his never having missed a shift. He had become somewhat brash with his own self-importance.

"Okay." Tidwell said his voice no longer tranquil. "I know you lied before and I know your lying now."

"Are you nuts?" Ohner leapt to his feet ready to walk out.

"Sit your ass down deputy," Tidwell shouted while rising to his feet. "You're in enough trouble as it is. Now sit down!" Ohner reluctantly returned to his seat. "Your lie cost people their lives. This isn't going away. You can do it the hard way or the easy way. It's your call. You know what I'm talking about now?"

"I have the right to remain silent," Ohner replied. Folding his arms across his chest he sat defiantly glaring at Tidwell. "And I have the right to have my union rep with me."

"So that's how you want to play it." Tidwell shook his head as he looked at the deputy. "Internal Affairs is on their way. You can hide behind the union, you can hide behind the constitution but you can't hide from the fact that I know you lied. I don't know why you did, I surely don't. You fell asleep, you were off somewhere getting laid, I don't know. But when you were suppose to be watching a murder suspect you weren't there and then lied and said you were. Son, your career is over. Hell, you may even go to jail for this. So before the I. A. thugs get here why don't you tell me what really happened?"

Ohner glared at his accuser. "I have the right to remain silent."

"Okay. Let me have your weapon," Tidwell ordered as the room's door swung open and the two Internal Affairs officer barged in. Called in on a holiday their frame of mind was less than affable. "He's all yours," Tidwell said. "But if I were you, I'd take his weapon before you do anything else."

CHAPTER TWENTY-FIVE

Rousseau declined Tidwell's request to have a conversation. The former suspect's telephone voice fluctuated between sociable and unsympathetic. Refusing to help, Rousseau continually repeated the name and phone number of his attorney. Tidwell thanked him and hung up. Tidwell did not fault him. Leaving only Lester he dialed the number. The mechanical recording informed him the line was disconnected. The uselessness of the number was not totally unexpected. Why not relocate? He was, after all, no longer considered a person of interest. Sensing he would have moved on if their positions were reversed Tidwell's only alternative was to drive out to the house. From there he could go home, a place he hadn't seen in three days.

Not expecting to find the house occupied Tidwell was astonished to see interior lights. At the front door he knocked loudly and stood patiently after hearing movement from within. The door was opened by a diminutive woman with long dark hair. Holding his badge so it was plainly visible he asked, "Mrs. Lester?" She nodded yes. After introducing himself Tidwell apologized for the late interruption, and then asked if her husband was home.

"He's gone," she replied.

"Gone?" Tidwell feared the worse. "When do you expect him back?"

"I don't," Tears formed in the woman's hazel eyes. "He abandoned me months ago. What's this about?"

"Mrs. Lester, may I come in? I know it's late. I won't stay long I promise. I just need to ask you some questions if that's alright." For a moment Mrs. Lester stood gawking at the Tidwell. Unsure what to do, she finally relented and stepped back, nodding consent.

Once inside Tidwell swept the room with his eyes. A sofa was centered in the room in front of a television. A single chair was situated to the side of the sofa and was accompanied by a small wooden table. The poorly upholstered chair offered the only individual place to sit. The television was a large screen and, as Tidwell entered the room, its volume was turned up louder than normal.

Crossing the room Mrs. Lester located the remote. Pushing a button she muted the program. "Sorry. It keeps me company," she apologized. "Please, have a seat." Settling into the sofa she left the chair for Tidwell. The faded house dress she wore clung tightly to her ample figure. Muscular arms and legs were evidence of her dedication to exercise.

"How long has your husband been gone?" Tidwell asked as he tried to make himself comfortable in the chair.

"I'm not really sure. Months I think." Mrs. Lester looked around the room avoiding his gaze. "He…. He ….. He really weren't my husband you know. Not in the church's eyes. We lived together and did everything married people do." She looked down. "You know what I mean. But I screwed it up and he left me."

"What happened?" Tidwell asked quietly. He was hopeful as to what she might know.

"I got knocked-up and he got mad. He made me get an abortion and have my tubes tied. Then he left me." Her voice cracked and she lowered her head. "I tried. I really did try. I just couldn't keep him happy and he left me. He didn't want any little monsters running around. That's what he called children you know - little monsters."

"Did he take anything with him?" Tidwell studied the woman's face. Trying to guess her age he thought her to be closer to a teenager than a mature woman.

"I don't know." Mrs. Lester looked up, her eyes surveying the room. "I really don't know what he took. He said he was going to work one day and he got in the car and drove off and I haven't seen him since."

"Does he have any friends or family that he would go to?" Tidwell leaned forward and rested his elbows on his knees.

"He knows a lot of people but I wouldn't call them friends, if you know what I mean." Tidwell didn't know what she meant but didn't ask for an explanation. "I don't know anything about family. He never talked about any."

Taking a deep breath Tidwell asked in a calming low voice, "Mrs. Lester, I think your husband has knowledge about something very bad. I need to talk to him so I can try and help him."

"What sort of bad?" At hearing the word bad, Mrs. Lester's eyes turned hard and burned into Tidwell's "What are you saying?"

"Do you remember the Cromwell murders?" The tone of Aaron's voice was casual, as if engaged in friendly conversation.

Mrs. Lester acknowledged she remembered with a nod of her head. "Do you think David had something to do with that?"

"That's what I am trying to find out," Tidwell said watching her expressions closely. Had she known about it all along? Was she an accessory? Was she the movie maker?

"That can't be." She insisted shaking her head in disbelief. "David is set in his ways and might be a hard man to understand and he might have a lot of needs and such, but I can't believe he could do something like that. No, no, no!" Tidwell thought she was about to cry but suddenly her expression shifted to one of defiance.

"Would you mind if I look around?" His request was delivered politely. "I could get a warrant but it's easier to have your permission."

"Is that really what you think? That David killed and raped those people?"

"I think he can help me find out who did," Tidwell answered all the while thinking he was positive Lester committed the crimes. "I really do think he can help me. Can I look around your house Mrs. Lester?"

Mrs. Lester's eyes hardened. Standing up, her hands on her hips she glared at him. "What are you looking for?" she demanded.

Tidwell eased himself from the chair. "You know, pictures, videos, weapons, and letters, anything that shows your husband can help us solve the case. Is there anything like that here? I know it's a lot to ask at this time of night. It really won't take long. "

She hesitated. Her eyes flashed as her mind digested what Tidwell had been saying. Softness almost returned to her face. "In the bedroom closet there's a trunk. David keeps pictures and such in it," she finally said. "There are some movies in there as well. He liked taking movies."

She lowered her head and plopped back to the sofa. All defiance vanished and when she spoke her voice was burdened with awkwardness. "I'm in some of those pictures Mr. Tidwell. I'm in some of the movies to. Your kind of folks won't understand that. I was just pleasing my husband. That's all. They weren't meant for anybody else but him and me. Is that hard to understand?" She looked away fixing her eyes on some spot on the ceiling.

"May I see them?" Tidwell realized he was on shaky ground. Her admission that they were unmarried could raise the validity of her entitlement to grant permission to search the trunk. "Please," he said.

Shaking her head she sat there and said nothing. Tidwell could only imagine her mind being tortured with apprehension. Her eyes betrayed her feeling of having said more than she should have. Mentally she wished David was there. He would not be flustered. He would know how to deal with this. At last she said, "Alright." She stood. "But you can't take anything with you. That's my right, right?"

Tidwell remained patient, the tone of his voice gentle. "Let's see what we are talking about before we cross that bridge."

"Come with me," Mrs. Lester commanded. After Tidwell stood she led him into the bedroom where she turned on the lights. Immediately catching Tidwell's attention was a nude portrait of Mrs. Lester. Prominently displayed above the bed, the painting was remarkable only for its seediness. Lacking artistic ability the painter failed to capture her real beauty. Instead an overzealous interpretation was given to the anatomy. The result was an amateurish rendition of large breasts and genitals.

Crossing the room she opened the closet door. Reaching inside she turned on the light and pointed to the corner. "Right there," she said.

She stepped back as Tidwell entered the closet. The majority of the clothing hanging from the wooden rods was female. A modest collection of shoes, also mainly female, lined the floor. At the rear of the room sat the aged trunk. Kneeling on the floor he shifted it towards him to allow room for its top to be opened. Holding his breath he lifted the top upward until it rested against the wall.

Colored photographs first caught his eye. Keeping his back to Mrs. Lester, who stood in the middle of the bedroom observing him, Tidwell lifted and examined picture after picture. Morality and social acceptance dictates a couples sex life be, for the most part, a private affair. The pictures he was now seeing destroyed that privacy. There were hundreds of them. Mrs. Lester was in a large percentage of them. But she was not alone in them.

On the glossy paper other men and women shared her spotlight. They were embracing each other. They were kissing each other. They were stroking each other. They were engaged in cunnilingus, fellatio, and masturbations. Every position one could fathom had been attempted and documented. Every angle was recorded. Partners and groups. It was undoubtedly why she was tentative about allowing anyone to view them. What struck Tidwell was the fact that David Allen Lester was not in any of the pictures.

Under the photographs he found videos. Some were commercial in nature, available at any adult store. Still in the distributors packing he scanned the titles. Those that were identifiable as being homemade he spent time examining for markings. Finding none he set them aside making a mental note as to the quantity and description. To take them, particularly with Mrs. Lester's mindset, a warrant would be needed. To the side of the videos, held together with ordinary twine, lay a bundle of envelopes, papers, and additional photographs. As he laid them with the videos Tidwell spied a small black fire proof box. Available for purchase at almost any store the box was unremarkable. Picking it up he discovered it was locked. "Do you know the combination?" he asked over his shoulder. Mrs. Lester shook her head no. "Do you know what is inside?" He turned to look at her in time to see her head shake.

Tidwell stood up and faced her. "I'm sorry but I'm going to have to get a warrant to take these things."

"Why?" Mrs. Lester's face flushed and her eyes filled with disbelief. "Those are private," she protested.

"I understand you're upset right now," Tidwell said attempting to calm her.

"Nobody is going to see those!" Her voice was a screech. "Those are mine and David's! You can't take them!"

"Mrs. Lester," Aaron said calmly. "You have to understand that we are going to take these items. We are going to do it legally with a warrant. Do you understand?"

"You are a bastard!" She screamed. Turning she fled from the room.

Reaching in his coat pocket Tidwell pulled out his cell phone and punched in the numbers to his office. When he was connected he issued instructions for a warrant, describing the trunk and its contents. He also wanted a warrant to search the remainder of the home and the barn. Relaying his fears that the material would be destroyed if he left, he told the desk officer he would remain until the warrant could be delivered. "Wake the judge up," he said to the deputy. "I know what day it is." He turned fleetingly to look at the contents of the trunk he left on the floor before squaring around to face the doorway. As he did he sensed more than saw Mrs. Lester's presence.

In the confines of the small closet the gunshot sounded like a massive explosion. Fire ripped through Tidwell's shoulder as he was knocked backwards by the impact of the bullet. Instinctively he reached for his holstered weapon. Fighting to stem the impending waves of shock his blurring eyes distinguished the form of Rhonda Lester across the bedroom holding a gun in preparation of firing again. Although a matter of seconds, the events played out in slow motion in his mind. He dropped the cell phone while reaching for his own weapon. Still connected the officer on the other end heard the first shot and before the second explosion alerted the entire force of the deputies currently on duty.

What the deputy couldn't know was that the second shot had come from Tidwell's weapon. His reflexes, before yielding to the pain and the shock, enabled him to draw and fire. Before knowing if his bullet hit its mark he passed out. Not totally accurate his bullet had nevertheless found its intended target. Striking Rhonda Lester in the chest, the impact knocked her from her feet. She lay motionless on the floor of her bedroom. As the minutes ticked by both Tidwell's and Lester's pools of blood increased in size.

Drifting in and out of consciousness Tidwell thought he heard distant sirens. Praying he was not hallucinating and that they were coming for him he attempted to sit up. The action caused him to blackout again. When he reopened his eyes paramedics were attending to his wound. "How is Mrs. Lester?" he mouthed. When told she was being worked on he gave a slight nod.

"Just stay with us," the paramedic was saying. In the fog of pain Tidwell thought he heard something about a painful wound, missed major organs. Not life threatening, the bullet shattered the collar bone and lodged in his shoulder. There was more muddled speech about a hospital and needing surgical treatment. Then the fog of pain and shock completely swallowed him.

Having checked his bleeding and immobilized the shoulder from possible movement the paramedics began the process of sliding Tidwell out of the closet. Turning him on his side at the doorway they navigated him past the frame into the bedroom. Instantly ten hands lifted him to a waiting stretcher and within seconds he was being loaded into an ambulance. The fog lifted slightly. "Someone's calling your wife," "The Sheriff will meet us at the hospital."

Weakly he asked, "What about Mrs. Lester?"

"D.O.A." He couldn't hear them but saw their mouths form the letters. Realizing Mrs. Lester was dead struck him as violently as if he were shot a second time. Sorrow overrode the pain He silently cursed himself. "She bled out before we got here." He couldn't hear them. The words about a justifiable shoot also went unheard as they blended with the wail of the ambulance's siren. Somewhere in his fog filled mind Tidwell privately admitted he committed a cardinal sin. He ignored Lester's movements thinking her harmless.

The mistake proved fatal. Mrs. Lester was dead. Aaron Tidwell was being rushed to emergency surgery. No porno pictures could be worth that. Drifting towards another blackout he questioned what in that trunk was worth shooting a police officer? What was worth risking being shot? When he again opened his eyes Tidwell was surrounded by doctors and nurses. In the distance, beyond the double doors, he thought he glimpsed his wife.

CHAPTER TWENTY-SIX

When Tidwell awoke he was in pain. His throat was raw, irritated by the five hours of plastic tubing forced down it during surgery. Memory told him he had been shot. Pain, then anesthetize, blocked out the rest. Still under the effects of the latter his vision was blurred. Shapes were fuzzy and distorted. He thought he saw someone standing next to the bed. He wasn't sure. It was problematical. Knowing he was no longer aware of his surroundings added to his discomfort. Through his haze he thought he detected a voice. His ears continued to ring from the decibels of the gunshots. He felt someone touch him. Instinctively he recoiled. The fog returned and he slept.

Hours later he opened his eyes. The pain caused him to grimace. Blinking several times the fuzziness cleared allowing him to survey the room. Seeing he was connected to monitors solicited a frown. Inserted then tapped to his arm was a needle attached to a tube. His eyes followed upward to the source; a translucent bag filled with equally transparent fluid. The roughness of his throat prevented an expletive from being uttered. Looking down the bed he saw her standing at the foot. Her gaze was fixed on his face. Awkwardly he smiled.

"You gave us a scare Tidwell," his wife said softly.

"I can't hear you." His words were hoarse, barely loud enough to be heard. His lips were dried but he could find no spittle in his mouth to wet them.

Moving to his side his wife leaned over to be close to his face. "You're going to be alright."

"I can't hear." Tidwell looked at her for acknowledgement that she understood him. "My ears are ringing."

She nodded. Over emphasizing her lips to form the words she spoke slowly. "The doctor says that will pass in a couple of days. You're going to be okay. Do you understand?"

With effort he nodded. "Pain," he mumbled.

"Okay. I'll go find a nurse." Squeezing his hand she left the room.

Recuperation was not Tidwell's forte. He was despondent. He was depressed at the forced idleness, depressed over the slow healing process, and depressed for the sake of being depressed. Having coerced his wife into retrieving Sawyer's journal from his desk drawer he sought sanctuary within the pages. Occasionally he would call those deputies still inclined to share information. Brief in nature, the conversations were provisional distractions from his misery. The conversations were not whispered sentences laced with guarded details of briskly changing events. Comprehensive details of pertinent proceedings were printed daily in the local papers. To the annoyance of the hovering Mrs. Tidwell he read them repetitively until, becoming angered, he hurled them across the room. Curses spewed from his mouth. Perhaps more than he himself, his wife pleaded for his return to work. With reservations, after six weeks, the doctors cleared him for duty.

Although back at his desk his injury still irritated him. His disposition had no chance of improvement. No one dared to make light of his situation or joke about the circumstances. Those thoughts were promptly discouraged by the gaze in his eyes. They were also curtailed by the knowledge he must appear before the shooting board. Their findings would, at the end of the day, determine if criminal charges would be required. Confident the board would arrive at a finding of justification was immaterial in his mind. Only the fact that Lester was gone was relevant. That fact was vital. That fact and one other fact - no one had any inkling to his whereabouts.

After Tidwell and Rhonda Lester exchanged gunfire the Lester home was dissected. Hospitalized, Tidwell missed the search, an aspect of the past few weeks that persistently embittered him. The trunk contained more than nude pictures of consenting adults. Besides being a trove of evidence connecting Lester to the Cromwell murders the aging trunk also contained videos of the murders committed in Arkansas, Colorado, and Virginia. Only documentation of the South Carolina murders was missing. Logic suggested that crime was committed after he abandoned his wife. Doubt of Lester's innocence had been everlastingly erased. In addition to the videos, a list containing five names and addresses was found. Checked against the names of the known victims, the list was assumed to be a to-do list for future home invasions. Geographically spread throughout the south and west it was inconceivable for Jackson County to offer protection to residents outside the boundaries of its jurisdiction. Making copies for official files, the list was sent to the FBI.

Not recovered was the gun used to murder Adam Cromwell and the other males. Small quantities of ammunition, along with the gun used by Rhonda Lester were located in the house. Naturally assuming that Lester took the weapon with him the words armed and dangerous were added to the official statement released to the press. Law enforcement agencies across the nation were advised to use caution when approaching the suspect.

By four in the afternoon on his first day back Tidwell finished reading the files compiled during his rehabilitation. Reserving the collection of newspaper clippings for last he briefly scanned the articles detailing the shooting. In his memory the event was still fresh and dramatic. Needing no synopsis of that night, his reading was more obligatory than purposeful.

"Are you ready?" The voice distracted him and he looked up to see the Sheriff standing by his desk.

"What?" Tidwell asked.

"Are you ready?" The Sheriff repeated. "You know for the shooting board?"

Tidwell shook his head. "Yes. I've still got some time. They don't meet until six."

"Do you need me to go with you?" The Sheriff's tone betrayed the sincerity of the words.

"Thank you." For a moment Tidwell considered replying in the affirmative. That reply would have been untruthful and uttered in spitefulness. "No thanks," he finally said. "I can handle it."

Noticeably relieved the Sheriff blathered something about being there for his men. "Good luck," was all that Tidwell understood as his boss walked away.

Turning his attention back to the clippings he managed to finish them before having to leave. With twenty-five minutes to spare he stood, stretched as best he could without causing pain to his shoulder, then put on his suit jacket. Tidwell shut off the light at his desk and entered the hall. Walking briskly to the far end he took the stairs and made his way to the bottom floor. He pushed through the door at the end of the stairs, walked down the corridor, and took a seat in the straight-backed chair at the end of the hallway. Quietly he waited.

Precisely at six the door was opened from the inside. "Detective Aaron Tidwell." The clerk spoke softly but plainly.

"Here," Tidwell responded as he stood and entered the room. The room was not strange to him. He had been in it several times during happier times for happier ceremonies. The furnishings were arranged to accommodate the proceedings. At one end was a long table. Chairs for the five member review board were positioned between the table and the wall. In front was a smaller table with a single chair facing the board. At the opposite end of the room sat another small table and chair, for use by the clerk. Instructed to sit at the smaller table, Tidwell crossed the room and settled onto the chair.

As he did a side door opened. The five members of the review board filtered in, taking their positions in front of the detective. Speaking first, the president of the board outlined the purpose of the hearing. "In the matter of the shooting death of Rhonda Lester," he said. Quickly he named those present in the room. "Do you wish to make an opening statement Detective Tidwell?"

"No sir." Tidwell answered sitting erect with his eyes fixed on the speaker. Having worked with them on a daily basis he knew every member on a first name basis.

"Very well," the board's president continued. Opening the file in front of him he cleared his throat. "Detective Tidwell, can you explain to the board why you were at the Lester home when you shot Rhonda Lester?"

The board already knew the answer. Tidwell was questioned in the hospital and again during his convalescence, the transcripts of both interviews lay in the files each member of the panel had in front of them. Still, he answered with a calm dispassionate voice. He repeated the reasons for his visit, his surprise that the house was occupied, and an abridgment of the conversations which transpired between him and Rhonda Lester.

"She willingly allowed you admittance to the home?" one board member asked.

"Yes sir, that is correct."

"And Rhonda Lester willingly allowed you to search the trunk in the bedroom closet of her home?"

"That is correct." Tidwell answered.

"At what point," the Chief of Detectives wanted to know, "Did she retract that permission?"

"At no point did Mrs. Lester retract her permission." Frustrated he was forced to answer the same question for a third time, Tidwell sat with his eyes straight ahead.

"At what point did Rhonda Lester's nature become hostile?" A close political ally of the Sheriff, the Chief of Detectives was a plump man with tendencies of resentment towards others who did not share his political views.

"When Mrs. Lester shot me. That's when her nature became hostile." Tidwell's voice was matter of fact.

"And before that Detective, did she ask you to leave? By your own testimony you were there only with her consent. You were in the bedroom closet only with her consent. Did she ever ask you to leave her home?" The Chief of Detectives sneered as he questioned Tidwell.

"She did not."

"Detective," The Chief Detective persisted. "Isn't it true that at some point she became irritated?"

"Yes, that is correct." Tidwell looked each board member in the eye as he spoke. "When I informed her I was obtaining a search warrant to remove the items in the trunk. At that point she became upset."

"Why then did you simply not leave? Were you looking for a confrontation?" The question from one of the watch commanders was expected by Tidwell. He had been asked the question numerous times in numerous ways.

"No, I was not. The trunk contained what I thought, and what has since proven to be, important evidence in the murders of the Cromwell family."

"So you did not believe yourself to be in danger?" The watch commander quizzed.

"Not until she shot me," Tidwell said.

The Chief of Internal Affairs picked up the questioning. "Detective, what was your state of mind that evening?"

"I was tired," Tidwell admitted

"You were tired? You had been on duty for over forty-eight hours. You were aggravated by the case. You just questioned a fellow deputy and accused him of making false statements. Would it be fair to say that you were angry?"

"With myself, yes."

"Would it be fair to say that you were also angry at the deputy?" The Chief of Internal Affairs glanced at the file in front of him.

"That would be a reasonable statement," Tidwell conceded.

"And would it be reasonable to say that you were also angry at Rhonda Lester?" The questioner looked up from the file waiting for the response.

Tidwell did not hesitate in responding. "No, that would not be a fair statement. Until she shot me I had no feelings towards Rhonda Lester. I had just met her for the first time."

"Would you admit your actions that evening were less than professional?"

"I would not." Outwardly Tidwell remained calm and patient as he endured the interrogation.

With varying degrees each member of the shooting board owed the Sheriff a certain amount of fidelity. Little effort was made to conceal the fact the Sheriff wanted Tidwell dismissed from the force. To do so he needed a legitimate platform. To him the shooting presented the perfect opportunity. In the end the Sheriff's objective was thwarted.

By a vote of three to two the board ruled the shooting justified. Aaron Tidwell was returned to full duty status. There would be no criminal charges filed. There would be no suspension. His service weapon was returned. Driving home after the board adjourned he felt little relief. Since seeing him in the hospital his wife initiated pressure on him to resign. Gentle suggestions at first, the suggestions intensified into introduction of raised voices. She would feel vindicated by the justified ruling but not with the return to duty. A fraction of him understood her fear. A part of him felt betrayed. A piece of him had made a start on the path in favor of her position. Minuscule as the thought was, he kept it to himself.

Special Agent Eileen Donner of the FBI appeared at the desk of Aaron Tidwell. He looked up and smiled. Having no contact with her since his briefing in her office he was astonished to see her. "Agent Donner," he said. "To what do I owe the pleasure?"

Donner returned his smile. "Is there someplace we can speak?" She looked around. "Privately I mean."

"Of course," he answered. Standing up he led her into an interrogation room and closed the door behind her. "Will this do?"

"It's perfect," she said still smiling. "That list your office sent us has proven to be quite helpful."

"Good!" Tidwell was pleased something positive had happened.

"Because of it we now have ten child molesters in custody. We owe that to you, Aaron."

Tidwell settled on the top of the table. "Why do I feel there is a but coming?" he asked her.

Donner flashed her ever present smile in his direction. "But," she said through the smile. "That was just the tip of the iceberg."

Tidwell held up his right hand. "Let me guess," he said. "You can't get any of them to flip on the others?"

"Actually," She paused. "We have something better and I wanted you to be the first to know."

Tidwell's face twisted into a massive question mark. "What could be better than members of the society? That's where this whole damn thing started, remember? What's better than having its members in custody?"

Donner hesitated, the smile faded from her lips. At once she was all business. "What I'm about to say can not leave this room, understood?" Her eyes, no longer shining, bore into his. "Understood?"

It was Tidwell's turn to delay. Something in her posture made him unsettled. "Understood," he finally uttered.

"We have Lester in custody." Donner spoke the words calmly but quickly.

The words stunned Tidwell. His face flushed with anger. There was murder in his eyes. "What the fuck are you talking about!" he demanded.

"David Allen Lester is in Federal custody. And," she pointed a finger in Tidwell's direction, "and he will remain in Federal custody."

"On what charges?" Tidwell was on his feet towering over the short Donner.

"Distribution and possession of child pornography."

"Are you insane?" Tidwell's anger was racing to a boiling point. "That's a state offense and you know it."

"Not when he distributes it through the U. S. mail." Donner stood her ground against the looming Tidwell. "Remember, he sent the tape to Gonzales through the mail. That's federal. Not to mention interstate flight and several other charges."

Still glaring Tidwell retook his perch on the table top. "How long have you had him?" he wanted to know.

"Three weeks," Donner said as her eyes softened yet showed no sign of amusement. "If it makes you feel any better he turned himself in to us after bartering a deal."

Tidwell felt a new wave of hostility flood his mind. "What deal?"

"He stays in Federal custody and he helps us put Utopia out of business. Christ Tidwell, he knows more about them than they do about themselves. The girls win and that's all that counts. It went all the way to the top. Command approved it. For the greater good."

Tidwell took a deep breath. Exhaling as he slowly stood up he walked around the room running his hands through his hair. His ambivalent feelings about retirement metamorphosed into full blown disgust with the job. "When do we get him?"

"You don't." Donner's words were cemented with finality.

"Ever?" Tidwell looked at Donner with incredulity. "I can't believe anyone would let that happen. It just doesn't make sense."

"Never," she said sighing, her shoulders briefly sagging. "It's over detective. It's best to let it go."

"Fifteen dead and he doesn't have to answer for it. What kind of justice is that Agent Donner?"

She shrugged. "Every day we cut deals with murders in order to catch a bigger fish. Do you know how many mafia hit men responsible for multiple deaths there are in witness protection? Of course you don't but the number would amaze you. As I said, it is for the greater good. It's always for the greater good of society. It always has been and always will be. You have been a cop long enough to know that." Donner's smile returned. "There is a bright side to this."

Tidwell stopped his pacing. "What possible bright side could there be?"

"You can close your case. He confessed to the murders. In a few weeks we will be forwarding the transcripts of the confessions. After that this conversation will no longer be classified as off the record." Her smile was accompanied by a twinkle in her eyes. "There is one more thing."

"What's that?"

"David Allen Lester wants to see you."

CHAPTER TWENTY-SEVEN

Winton, North Carolina is not special. The small compact town with a population of less than one thousand is non-descript. Fame has eluded the hamlet. True, it is the county seat. And true, the Chowan River cuts through the northeastern boundary. But the asphalt of the three highways to the west is not filled with vacationers determined to spend their time and money on the lure of a city with no attractions. Instead the highways are traversed by the local population and supplemented by the occasional big rigs making deliveries to the town's markets. The traffic is also supplemented by visitors to the Federal correctional facility located southeast of the city on River Road. Simply named CI Rivers, the minimum security penitentiary is manned and operated through contracts with private companies. The arrival of its newest resident, David Allen Lester, passed without fanfare or attendance of the media.

Accompanied by Special agents of the FBI, Lester arrived, handcuffed and shackled, during the early morning hours of darkness. Shuffled into reception he was stripped, searched, photographed, and fingerprinted. Given inmate number 695837, he underwent delousing then, minus belt and shoe strings, was ordered to dress in white prison garments. Placed in solitary confinement his cell measured eight feet by six feet. Attached to one wall was a steel bunk with a thin mattress, a single pillow, two sheets, and a single blanket. Attached to the opposite wall were the stainless steel toilet and sink. Meals were slid through the bars, the trays retrieved exactly one hour later.

Strictly supervised Lester shuffled in shackles to and from daily exercise. Secluded from the general population, the hour outside his cell was monitored by blank faced armed guards who abstained from any speech. He didn't mind the lack of conversation. Lifting his face skyward he would gulp deeply, taking in as much of the fresh open air as possible. Television and radio privileges were withheld. Writing paper, envelopes, and pens were issued on a controlled basis. Outside visitation was denied. The only exception was the periodic FBI agent sent to question him. Usually the interrogations gobbled away hours at a time. As a means of escape, and with few interruptions to prevent it, he retreated into the world of fantasy he created in his mind. It was there he found solace. It was there he lived free and complete, satisfying exaggerated cravings. A lullaby to his being, he used those thoughts at night to drift into sleep. Each morning he repeated the routine.

Informed of Tidwell's impending visit Lester smiled. There were, however, stipulations to the meeting. With a wave of his hand he assured them of his conformity even before hearing them. "I have done nothing but oblige you. Why do you think I would grant anything but the same to him?" he asked.

The prospect of breaching the daily monotony lifted his spirits. Mentally he calculated the hours remaining before he could speak with his visitor. Psychologically perceptive, the understanding that he would be expected to communicate his account and raison d'être of the past six years did not upset him. Viewing the obligation as emancipation, his mind formulated the words he would say, fixed the tone of voice he would use and determined the facial expressions he would display. Rehearsing in his cell he performed the parts of both characters - the inmate and the detective. Pretending to be Tidwell, he asked the questions he thought would be asked. His voice, modified with what he thought appropriate nuances, answered the questions quickly. Always a believer in formulating plans he tore apart his thoughts. Discarding those he sensed ineffective he memorized those most durable. Practice, practice, practice. His mind burned with energy. Finally confident he had equipped himself for the meeting he awaited the appointed hour. Like a newborn he slept with tranquility.

Shuffling in his shackles Lester was escorted into the visitor's room. Greeted by the waiting table and chairs he hurried to them. Tidwell had not yet arrived and he wanted to be seated before he did. Impatiently he stood while his shackles were released. Forced into the chair, his wrists were handcuffed to the table, his ankles to the floor. Satisfied with their work the blank faced guards took their positions in the room's corners. Like statuettes they stood frozen, seemingly melting into the walls.

Tidwell entered without fanfare. Crossing the room he occupied the chair facing Lester. Suppressing his surprise he sat quietly studying the inmate. Since incarcerated Lester reasoned it unnecessary to continue the practice of shaving his head. The short black hair altered Lester's appearance, the face was somehow softer. The growth of beard, blackish gray, hid the square of the jaws. Only the eyes were as he had remembered them. Still, the alteration of the head and face was shocking to Tidwell. He hoped his face hadn't bared his thoughts.

"This must be a surprise to you," Lester said. "Seeing me chained like a wild beast. I'm sure it is shocking." Lester looked for a reaction but found none. "It is shocking to me as well." He sighed. "But what was I to do? My options were limited and the ever relentless Aaron Tidwell was on the hunt as well as many others. The deal with federal authorities is insurance. I continue to live and my enemies are prevented from inflicting unnecessary harm." He stopped and smiled. "May I call you Aaron? I feel like we are old friends. And, please, call me David. There is no need for formalities at this juncture."

"You agreed to answer my questions. I'm not here to be your buddy." Tidwell stated his eyes drilled into Lester's.

"So, you shall not be. Not today, nor any day," Lester retorted. "Still," he smiled again, his voice dropping an octave. "We are irrefutably linked for perpetuity by circumstances. You are blameless in this relationship but linked nonetheless. Buddies or not, we are bound with unbreakable ties. Unbreakable even in death, the bond passed from generation to generation."

To Tidwell's knowledge Lester had no children. He let the statement pass with out comment. Instead he turned to the subject of Caleb Rousseau. Asking about their relationship he pressed the prisoner for details.

Lester's smile beamed. "That was brilliant, don't you think?" He uttered a short deep laugh. "Not without risk mind you, but brilliant nonetheless. If your deputy had been awake it would have been futile."

"The deputy was sleeping?" Tidwell asked.

"Like a new born." Lester's eyes danced with the memory. "He must have been a tired fellow. He was still asleep when I returned. I saluted him as I drove past. Ironic, the situation he allowed himself to be trapped in. The truth would have resulted in my apprehension but cost the lad his employment. His alternative was to lie. I was comfortable putting fate in the hands of human nature. I was not disappointed. We deceive ourselves into thinking we are more than mortals. We deceive ourselves into believing we have the power to rise above our natural instincts. Such erroneous beliefs pounded into our minds by teachers, preachers, supervisors, and yes, even our spouses; yet in reality, in a crisis, we all revert back to our natural propensity. Everybody lies to make themselves look good." He paused. "How is the lad doing?"

"Why Rousseau?" Tidwell questioned while fighting his urges to reach across the table and take Lester by the throat. The convict's haughtiness angered the detective.

Lester's smile evaporated. "He is deserving," he responded. The voice was flat, without emotion. "Supercilious attitude. Gifted with certain attributes but cursed with unawareness." Tidwell harbored the same thoughts about Lester. "Life is plump with opportunities. The distinction between those with intelligence and those who chose to remain ignorant is the failure to embrace those opportunities. Rousseau's life and mine were analogous. We were both raised by liberated relatives who assumed the powerful responsibility to indoctrinate us into the world of sexual gratification. The only difference was he lived in Louisiana and I in Iowa. Life led us to the same place at the same instance. Ancestry provided us with similar appearances. I acknowledged the opportunity those facts presented. He did not. His failings made him the perfect pawn. When I discovered he lived in the same county as I, the ability to manipulate events was elementary. Gonzales' feelings towards Rousseau made him an enthusiastic contributor to the design." Lester shrugged. A whimsical expression came over his face.

"An unforeseen accident obliged an early execution of the plan. Who could have foreseen that Alberto would take the life of a rookie police officer? Happenstance."

"Let me understand this," Tidwell said. "You and Rousseau. Same type of childhood. Same looks. Same employment. Same friends. And you end up in the same county. I'd call that more than just chance. I'd also say it is really hard to believe."

"Truth is always stranger than fiction." Lester smiled briefly then became serious "Are you a religious man?" Not waiting for a response he continued. "I believe that God is overwhelmed with responsibility. To reduce those responsibilities he created a specific number of molds for us mortal beings. We all fit into one of those molds. Although God is the epitome of perfection his molds are flawed with imperfections. If mortals were perfect there would be no purpose for a God. Is that so problematic to comprehend?

"Caleb Rousseau and I are not unaccompanied in the mold we share. It is naïveté to view our childhood experiences as isolated circumstances. Does anyone really know what transpires behind the privacy of a closed door? It is denial to think heightened cravings for sexual pleasures are confined to a handful of individuals. That notion is lunacy.

"Society continues its attempt to impede what God bequeathed. Abstinence is not natural or healthy. Society commands that copulating be restricted to approved positions and confined to the darkness of the nation's bedrooms. Religious leaders spew eternal damnation for pleasuring one's self. While gushing with sermons on God's beauty and how we are created in his image they demand our flesh be hidden under unflattering baggy clothing. The force of those words and the imposed restrictions give support to the tendency for corpulent self-mutilation of our bodies. Yet even those hold a spattering of beauty. Reduced to inhibitions we dwell in fear of our one true liberation, our one true equalizing natural ability. Affluent or impoverished the ritual is indistinguishable. Only in this are all humans equal. Yet to embrace this analysis means certain persecution, certain bigotry, and certain banishment. When will we educate ourselves and abolish our arcane apprehension concerning sex?"

Tidwell endured the rhetoric. Buried within the words lay the crux of Lester's mental reasoning. Yet, through the discourse he detected no shame for his beliefs or his actions. Instead, the dialogue directed towards society what Lester considered the disgrace of impeding sexual freedom and liberation. For someone who had not finished high school and had no college education, Lester was remarkably articulate, his intelligence astounding but ill-directed. Controlled by urges and desires the genius of his mind twisted rational and misinterpreted justification for his actions. Secretly Tidwell prayed that there were not other Lester's scattered among the populations of the world.

"Tell me what happen at the Cromwell's." Tidwell's words ended a long silence in which the two men occupied themselves by unblinkingly staring into each others faces.

Lester constricted his lips and nodded his head. "Yes, of course. That's why you are here, is it not? Yes. You have a right to know. Like I, you have relived it repeatedly for a long period." He paused to look around the room. Letting his eyes rest on the guards momentarily he returned his gaze to Tidwell. "I held such great expectations that evening," he said. His voice was low and soft. "Such great expectations." He paused again.

"I found them where I anticipated, in the bedroom, engaged in intercourse. The women were as magnificent as I imagined. God sanctified both with unfettered power over the male species. For a moment I did nothing but revel in their movements, inhaling the bouquet of their scent. When I made my presence known they were tentative, understandably apprehensive to what was to come.

"I calmed their reservations by talking with them about their membership in Utopia. They had been members for four years. The information for me was not new. I was privy to that knowledge for quite sometime. Amanda came to them shortly afterwards, through the conventional sequence developed by the firm in Canada. Promising that no harm would come to them I gained enough of their confidence to secure their collaboration. Joyce, with my direction, obligingly restrained Adam. Amanda continued to show signs of nervousness and I stroked her hair to console her. Oh what hair it was; silken under my fingers, its fragrance of night blooming jasmine wafting in my nostrils, its sheen that of shimmering gold. Touching her awakened my desires."

Tidwell bit the inside of his bottom lip in an attempt to prevent any expression from showing on his face. Lester was visibly enjoying the telling of that night's events, and Tidwell was determined not to add to that enjoyment by revealing his loathing. He had repeatedly watched the tape sent to Gonzales, looking for evidence. He had also viewed the tapes seized from Lester's trunk. Listening to Lester reinforced his sense of how horrendous the final hours must have been for the Cromwell's.

"The couple taught their ward well," Lester continued. "In return she thanked them by becoming a master in the performance of those subjects." Lester stopped and looked upward towards the ceiling his eyes glazed with remembrance. "Superior to the others, I thought I had finally found a worthy assemblage of humans. Those shared moments were cherished I thought by everyone. I know I did. I continue to witness them in my mind, as I continue also to listen to the whimper of their pleasure and the euphoria of their orgasmic screams. They were agreeable, submissive members participating in unique freedom and emancipation. I so wanted not to have to punish them." His eyes returned to rest on Tidwell.

"Ultimately their duplicitous objective was exposed." Lester's voice dropped all emotion and became monotone. "Never did they entertain intentions of my acceptance into their brotherhood. Truth, as it always will, betrayed them. Truth barred their release from a self-inflicted delusion of their sole entitlements to paradise. Their treachery was reprehensible - their transgressions punishable by death.

"I escorted Joyce and Amanda into the bathroom and began their purification. I had prepared a solution of chlorine and water preceding my arrival in the event it would be required. First Joyce, then Amanda, in turn, obliged with the feminine ceremony of douching. Afterward they rinsed their mouths. Leaving nothing to chance I employed the remaining solution on wash clothes and bathed their bodies. Satisfied with that fastidious phase of the purification process I supplied them with suitable lipstick. They were so beautiful. My hand trembled as I administered the adrenaline injections.

"Amanda was locked in the bathroom for her own safety. Joyce and I returned to the bedroom. Positioning her on the bed I recited her peccadillo, offered her redemption, then delivered her eulogy and, to speed the effects of the drug, pretended to strangle her. Compassionately I closed her gaping eyes.

"Adam had been constantly thrashing against his bonds, his actions disruptive and disrespectful to the sanctity of eternal deliverance. Calming him was uncomplicated. A single gunshot to the head and his conceited heroics ended.

"The use of the pistol before intended was inopportune. When I returned for Amanda she was panic-stricken; a combination of fear and knowledge. Her eyes welled with tears threatening to tarnish the sacrament of her purification. The drug stopped her heart there, in the bathroom. She alone held the most promise for development into an apostle of unhindered devotion and independence. Her punishment held no joy for me. Glumly I carried her form to the bedroom and laid her beside the others. Spreading her legs I placed the artificial rose between them, leaned over and kissed her forehead."

"And the fire?" Tidwell asked. "Why set the house on fire?"

"Insurance they would be discovered," Lester said. "Sterno is crude but effective."

Tidwell's eyes burned with disgust. "What about the flower? What twisted rational did it symbolize?"

Lester laughed the laugh of animated malice. "Brilliant was it not? How many wasted hours were spent deciphering the symbol of the flower?" He mocked Tidwell. "Did it represent the deflowering of the innocent? Or perhaps the loss of purity? And why an artificial flower and not a real one?" Lester's laughter filled the room.

"How predictably conventional humans are! How many man-hours in how many states have been frivolously wasted?" Abruptly he stopped laughing. Like a teacher denigrating a student who failed to comprehend an obviously simple equation, Lester spoke in a patronizing tone. "My dear Aaron, the flower signified naught. A mere postscript intended as a capricious mystery for the great minds of perception. I see now that its purpose was achieved."

Tidwell stood and turned his back on Lester. Anger and aggravation mingled with nausea and flushed his face. Standing quietly he allowed the minutes to pass as he regained his composure. His back still to the prisoner he spoke, "Are you aware that Rhonda is dead?" Turning, he faced Lester not expecting to see any reaction from someone as callous as the inmate. He was not disappointed.

Lester's face remained empty. "Yes," he answered. "I am aware of her demise. Regrettable as it may be it is understandable. She was strong willed and illogical at times. Her aptitude for embracing a liberal existence was, at one point extraordinary. Life's journey eroded her enthusiasm, deceived her receptiveness. Incompetent with her self maintenance, her habits evolved into tawdriness. No longer sympathetic toward enlightening life she became superfluous. I was left with no alternative but to abandon her. Life offers varying choices. Her choices were not always the most judicious."

Lester stopped and examined Tidwell's face. There was something he could not quite put his finger on. Was it a wrinkle on his brow? Perhaps it was a quivering of the lips. A possible flaring of the nostrils. Or was it sadness in the eyes? Perhaps it was an amalgamation of all of those things. Slowly he grinned. "Her death burdens you with distress. Accountability is a burden for those lacking intensity of conviction. Appease your soul Aaron. I harbor no acrimony for you. She was always irrational."

Darkness had replaced daylight by the time Tidwell emerged from the prison and made his way to his car. He sat behind the wheel and jammed a cigar between his teeth. Lost in thought, he sat immobile as he twirled the tobacco in his mouth. Two years had vanished since he first saw the lifeless bodies of the Cromwell's. That day distorted his life. Sleepless nights, fatigue, anger, and frustration had inflicted disenchantment upon his perceptions. Besides casting doubt on his professional aptitude and inflicting physical pain, the manhunt caused an estrangement with his wife. In the end it was all for naught. Theoretical greater good denied fifteen victims of homicide any possible validity. In this enlightened world how could anyone portray that outcome as justice? Reaching into his jacket pocket he found a lighter. A flick of his thumb produced a flame and he lit the cigar. He started the engine and backed out of the parking space to begin the long ride home.

EPILOGUE

Built on the northwestern shore of Lake Ontario, Toronto is Canada's largest and most diversified city. Of the city's two and a half million residents nearly one half were born somewhere other than Canada. Culture, arts, and theater abound in the sprawling metropolis, as does ethnic communities; the eighty plus enclaves representations from around the globe. Consistently ranked one of the world's cleanness and secure, it is not, however, without crime, a fact Reginald Dunlittle knew only to well. An inspector with the Royal Canadian Mounted Police, he witnessed first hand the seediness those in the tourism business desperately tried to hide. Yet, even he was not aware of everything until the FBI contacted Canadian authorities with information provided by an inmate in their custody. The information kicked off a six month investigation; an investigation that was, Dunlittle hoped, about to end.

Dressed in tattered and dirty clothing normally associated with someone homeless, Reginald Dunlittle shuffled up and down Gifford Street watching the three story gray stoned building bearing the sign Imports/Exports. As he moved, his arms thrashed through the air and his facial expressions, reminiscent of a lack of sanity, were menacing enough to keep those passing by at a distance. Talking to no one his voice fluctuated between obnoxious and barely audible. The wig of matted hair protruding from the faded baseball cap concealed the radio receiver in his ear. Less than a block away his every word was recorded, his every movement taped. Occasionally a somber voice in his ear would direct him one way or another. It was a routine he participated in for a week.

"On your toes," the voice said in his ear. Looking up Dunlittle saw the black town car slowly come up the street. "This maybe our pigeon," the voice said. "Hallelujah!" Dunlittle shouted several times as he made his way towards where he knew the car would stop. "Hallelujah! Hallelujah! He is coming!"

Slowing to a crawl the car pulled to the curb. Dunlittle, reaching the front of the vehicle continued his jumbled diatribe. Leaning over the fender he began shouting at his reflection and running his hands over the metal. The rear doors of the car opened quickly. A short man, barely five foot, with a balding head and hazel green eyes slipped from the car and hurried towards Dunlittle. "Get away from the car you idiot!" he screamed.

"Now is the time for all God's men!" Dunlittle shouted. "All God's men!"

"Are you crazy? Get away from the car or I'll call the police!" The short man was a foot away from Dunlittle. Looking up Dunlittle emitted a robust laugh. In a single motion he stood, extended his arm, and grabbed the man by the back of the neck. Fear flooded the man's eyes. "Let go of me," he demanded. Another swift motion sent the man crashing into the side of the car.

"Christopher Tolliver," Dunlittle said in a stern voice. "You're under arrest for human trafficking. Do you understand?"

"Get your hands off of me you fool," Tolliver said. "You have made a mistake!"

"No sir," answered Dunlittle, "It is you that has made the mistake." By the time Dunlittle reached the end of the sentence Gifford Street was flooded with police. "We have a warrant to search your office building and your home. Do you understand?" Dunlittle turned his prisoner over to uniformed officers who handcuffed him then led him away.

With ten other officers Dunlittle entered the building. The first floor offices were typical of any respectable business; desks, filing cabinets, computers, copy machines and a conference room. The three secretaries were escorted briskly to the sidewalk and into the arms of waiting Mounties. At the back of the first floor hallway a staircase led upward. Taking the steps three at a time Dunlittle was first to reach the landing. Pushing through the double doors he found himself in an unfurnished vestibule with large black and white tiles. Directly ahead another set of stairs led to the top floor. On both sides of the foyer double metal door with black and red warning signs saying RESTRICTED - NO ADMITTANCE were chained and padlocked. "Open those," Dunlittle ordered as he began his climb up the stairs.

The third floor was one room. With out windows it appeared smaller than its actual size. The east end contained a dormitory style bath room with multiple toilets and multiple shower heads. At the west end of the room stood rusting washers and dryers. In the center of the room, at evenly spaced intervals, stood the metal cots. There were twenty four in total. Twelve were occupied by young girls chained to the bed's railings. As Dunlittle rushed from the stairs their eyes were wide with fear. He stopped and stared at each girl. "My dear God," he said his voice almost a whisper. Collecting himself he cleared his throat. "Its okay ladies," he told them. "I'm with the Mounties. Everything will be okay. No one will ever hurt you again."

For his cooperation David Allen Lester was granted additional privileges. After eleven months he was transferred from isolation to the less restrictive life of the prison's general population. His access to televisions and newspapers, and his continued interviews with federal agents, allowed him to follow the on going capture of Utopia members. Tearing each article from the papers, he used them to decorate the walls of his cell. When informed of the Mounties raid in Toronto, he laughed uncontrollably.

"Pride goes before the fall," he said. "I am confident they are no longer flaunting their haughtiness of sole entitlement. Well done gentlemen. Well done." For the most part he remained quite and reclusive, but cooperative with guards, who considered him a model prisoner.

Easily talking his way into being assigned a job in the carpenter's shop, Lester adapted to his confinement. The adaptation, he knew, was necessary for his plans. Having greater access to the prison and its grounds, he studied the construction of the buildings, the schedule of arriving and departing vehicles, and the strength and weakness of each guard.

Always disciplined and meticulous he formulated his idea without hurry. His right to use the carpenters tools added to his assurance that when the time arrived his objective would be reached. But before that time, he was content with a course of watching and learning.

An early blast of snow and cold the day before Thanksgiving provided his opportunity. Standing in the doorway of the shop he watched the garbage truck as it moved towards the dumpster. The guards, normally hovering nearby were, instead, huddled indoors away from the wind. The vision of the tower guards would, he knew, be blocked from the right side of the truck for two minutes as the hydraulic cylinders lifted the metal container above the truck.

Slowly he stepped from the doorway. Casually he lifted his jacket collar around his neck. The wind was bitter, twirling snow through the air. Reduced visibility aided his efforts. Taking a last look around the yard he rushed forward. Reaching the right side of the truck he inched his way to the rear, slid around the back, and pulled himself onto the mound of trash. Shielding his head from the falling waste he listened to the harsh banging of metal against metal as the driver insured the bin was emptied. Nothing else fell on his head. Lester held his breath.

The driver shifted gears and Lester felt the truck going backwards. From one jacket pocket he pulled cotton balls and stuffed them into his nostrils. From the other pocket he pulled a wood file he had fashioned into a knife. The truck stopped. Gears were once again shifted. The truck lurched forward. Lester waited. At the gate the truck stopped, the driver spoke with the guards. Despite the cold, sweat beaded Lester's forehead. There was another lurch and the truck was moving through the gates. No one had braved the cold and checked the back. David Allen Lester was free.

Jackson County, North Carolina no longer held any attraction for Aaron Tidwell. Bowing to the wishes of his wife, he ended his career and turned in his badge and weapon. Disillusioned over the past two years and restless from no employment, he devoted his time to saving his marriage by agreeing to every suggestion presented by his wife. But in the end, his attempts were in vain. After the divorce, the former Mrs. Tidwell, in order to be closer to family, moved to Texas. Aaron

Tidwell traded the mountains of North Carolina for the seclusion of the mountains in Wyoming.

On Christmas Eve, as he was preparing for bed, his phone rang. "Tidwell," he said as he answered it.

"Merry Christmas, Aaron," the voice replied. "This is David Lester."

Tidwell sighed. "I heard you had escaped."

"Brilliant wasn't it," Lester bragged. "Rudimentary, but nonetheless brilliant."

"What do you want?" Tidwell demanded.

"Just to say I am sorry you are no longer my challenger. But, perhaps another time if you should be convinced to end your unfortunate early retirement. I would look forward to that immensely. Until then, I bid you ado."

The phone went dead in Tidwell's hand.